LOOK HOW
THE FISH LIVE

J·F·POWERS
LOOK HOW THE FISH LIVE

Alfred·A·Knopf   *New York*   1975

THIS IS A BORZOI BOOK
PUBLISHED BY ALFRED A. KNOPF, INC.

LIBRARY OF CONGRESS CATALOGING
IN PUBLICATION DATA
Powers, James Farl [date]   Look how the fish live.
CONTENTS: Look how the fish live.—Bill.—Folks.
[etc.]
I.   Title.
PZ3.P8743LO   [PS3566.O84]   813'.5'4   75–8237
ISBN 0–394–49608–6

"Keystone," "Bill," "Priestly Fellowship," and "Farewell" originally appeared in *The New Yorker*. "Look
How the Fish Live" first appeared in *The Reporter*.
"Folks" and "Moonshot" were first published in *The
Nation*. "Tinkers" first appeared in *American Re-
view*, "One of Them" in *The Critic*, and "Pharisees"
in *Commonweal*.

MANUFACTURED IN THE UNITED STATES OF AMERICA

FIRST EDITION

To Betty

CONTENTS

LOOK HOW
THE FISH LIVE

LOOK HOW
THE FISH LIVE

It had been a wonderful year in the yard, which was four city lots and full of trees, a small forest and game preserve in the old part of town. Until that day, there hadn't been a single casualty, none at least that he knew about, which was the same thing and sufficient where there was so much life coming and going: squirrels, both red and grey, robins, flickers, mourning doves, chipmunks, rabbits. These creatures, and more, lived in the yard, and most of these he'd worried about in the past. Some, of course, he'd been too late for, and perhaps that was best, being able to bury what would have been his responsibility.

Obviously the children had been doing all they could for some time, for when he happened on the scene the little bird was ensconced in grass twisted into a nesting ring, soggy bread and fresh water had been set before it—the water in a tiny pie tin right under its bill—and a birdhouse was only inches away, awaiting occupancy. Bird, food and drink, and house were all in a plastic dishpan.

"Dove, isn't it?" said his wife, who had hoped to keep him off such a case, he knew, and now was easing him into it.

"I don't know," he said, afraid that he did. It was a big little bird, several shades of grey, quills plainly visible because the feathers were only beginning. Its bill was black and seemed too long for it. "A flicker maybe," he said, but he didn't think so. No, it was a dove, because where were the bird's parents? Any bird but the dove would try to do something. Somewhere in the neighborhood this baby dove's mother was posing on a branch like peace itself, with no thought of anything in her head.

"God," he groaned.

"Where *are* the worms?" said his wife.

"We can't find any," said the oldest child.

"Here," he said, taking the shovel from her. He went and dug near some shrubbery with the shovel, which was probably meant for sand and gravel. With this shovel he had buried many little things in the past. The worms were deeper than he could go with such a shovel, or they were just nowhere. He pried up two flagstones. Only ants and one many-legged worm that he didn't care to touch.

He had found no worms, and when he came back to the bird, when he saw it, he was conscious of returning empty-handed. His wife was going into the house.

"That bird can't get into that house," he said. "It's for wrens."

"We know it," said the oldest child.

He realized then that he had pointed up an obvious difficulty that the two girls had decently refrained from mentioning in front of the bird and the two younger children, the boys. But he hadn't wanted them to *squeeze* the dove into the wrenhouse. "Well, you might as well leave it where it is. Keep the bird in the shade."

"That's what we're doing."

"We put him in the dishpan so we could move him around in the shade."

"Good. Does it eat or drink anything?"

"Of course."

He didn't like the sound of that. "Did you *see* it eat or drink anything?"

"No, she did."

"You saw it eat or drink?" he said to the younger girl.

"Drink."

"It didn't eat?"

"I didn't see him eat. He maybe did when we weren't watching."

"Did it drink like this?" He sipped the air and threw back his head, swallowing.

"More like this." The child threw back her head only about half as far as he had.

"Are you sure?"

"Of course."

He walked out into the yard to get away from them. He didn't know whether the bird had taken any water. All he knew was that one of the children had imitated a bird drinking—rather, had imitated him imitating a chicken. He didn't even know whether birds threw back their heads in drinking. Was the dove a bird that had to have its mother feed it? Probably so. And so probably, as he'd thought when he first saw the bird, there was no use. He was back again.

"How does it seem? Any different?"

"How do you mean?"

"Has it changed any since you found it?"

The little girls looked at each other. Then the younger one spoke: "He's not so afraid."

He was touched by this, in spite of himself. Now that they'd found the bird, she was saying, it would be all right. Was ever a bird in worse shape? With food it couldn't eat, water it probably hadn't drunk and wouldn't, and with a house it couldn't get into—and *them!* Now they punished him with their faith in themselves and the universe, and later, when these had failed and the bird began to sink, they would punish him some more, with their faith in him. He knew what was the best thing for the bird. When the children took their naps, then maybe he could do the job. He was not soft. He had flooded gophers out of their labyrinthine ways and beheaded them with the shovel; he had purged a generation of red squirrels from the walls and attic of the old house when he moved in, knowing it was them or him. But why did animals and birds do this to him? Why did children?

"Why'd you pick this bird up? Why didn't you leave it where it was? The mother might've found it then."

"She couldn't lift him, could she?"

"Of course not."

"Well, he can't fly."

"No, but if you'd left it where it fell, the mother might see it. The mother bird has to feed a baby like this." Why couldn't she lift it? Why couldn't the two parents get together and just put it back in the nest? Why, down through the ages, hadn't birds worked out something for such an emergency? As he understood it, they were descended from reptiles and had learned how to grow feathers and fly. The whale had gone to sea. But he didn't know whether he believed any of this. Here was a case that showed how incompetent nature really was. He was tired of such cases, of nature passing the buck to him. He hated to see spring and summer come to the yard, in a way. They meant death and mosquitoes to him.

It had been the worst year for mosquitoes that anyone could remember, and in Minnesota that was saying a lot. He had bought a spraying outfit, and DDT at $2.50 a quart, which, when you considered that there was no tax on it, made you think. A quart made two gallons, but he was surprised how quickly it went. The words on the bottle "Who enjoys your yard—you or the mosquitoes?" had stayed with him, however. He had engaged professionals, with a big machine mounted on a truck, to blow a gale of poison through the yard. (In other years, seeing such an operation in other yards, he had worried about the bees.) The squirrels and rabbits in residence had evacuated the trees and lily beds while he stood by, hoping that they and the birds understood it was an emergency measure. He believed, however, that the birds received too much credit for eating annoying insects. Wasps, he knew, consumed great numbers of mosquitoes—but what about *them?* The mosquito hawk, a large, harmless insect, was a great killer of mosquitoes, but was itself killed by birds—by martins. That was the balance of nature for you. Balance for whom? You had to take steps yourself—drastic steps. Too drastic?

"Now I want you to show me exactly where you found this bird."

The little girls looked at each other.

"Don't say anything. Just take me to the exact spot."

They walked across the yard as if they really knew where they were going, and he and the little boys followed. The girls appeared to agree on the spot, but he supposed the one was under the influence of the other. The older one put out a foot and said, "Here."

He hadn't realized they were being that exact. It was surprising how right they were. Fifty or sixty feet overhead, in a fork of a big white oak, he saw a nest, definitely a dove's nest, a jerry-built job if he ever saw one, the sky visible between the sticks, and something hanging down. He moved away and gazed up again. It was only a large dead leaf, not what he'd feared, not a baby bird hanging by its foot. He felt better about having had the yard sprayed. The machine on the truck was very powerful, powerful enough to bend back the bushes and small trees, but he doubted that it had blown the baby dove out of the nest. This was just an unusually bad nest and the bird had fallen out. Nature had simply failed again.

"The nest! I see it! See?"

"Yes." He walked away from them, toward the garage. He hadn't called the nest to their attention because restoring the bird was out of the question for him —it was a job for the fire department or for God, whose eye is on the sparrow—but that didn't mean that the children might not expect him to do it.

"Just keep the bird in the shade," he called from the garage. He drove down to the office, which he hadn't planned to visit that day, and spent a few hours of peace there.

And came home to another calamity. In the kitchen, the little girls were waiting for him. Something, they said, had jumped out of the lilies and pushed one of the young bunnies that hadn't been doing anything, just eating grass near the playhouse. A weasel, they thought. Their mother hadn't seen it happen, had only heard the bunny crying, and had gone up to bed. There was no use going to her. They were in possession of what information there was. He should ask them.

"Don't go out there!"

"Why not?"

"Mama says if the bunny has the rabies it might bite."

He stood still in thought. Most of his life had been spent in a more settled part of the country. There was a great deal he didn't know about wildlife, even about the red squirrel and the yellow-jacket wasp, with which he had dealt firsthand, and he knew it. He could be wrong. But there was something ridiculous about what they were suggesting. "Did you see whatever it was that pushed the rabbit?"

"Of course!" said the older girl. It was this that distinguished her from all others in the house.

"What did it look like?"

"It went so fast."

This was ground they'd covered before, but he persevered, hoping to flush the fact that would explain everything. "What color was it?"

"Kind of—like the rabbit. But it went so fast."

This, too, was as before. "Maybe it was the mama rabbit," he said, adding something new. The more he thought about it, the more he liked it. "Maybe she didn't want the young one to come out in the open—in the daytime, I mean. Maybe she was just teaching it a lesson." He didn't know whether rabbits did that, but he did know that this particular mother was intelligent. He had first noticed her young ones, just babies then, in a shallow hole alongside a tiny evergreen that he had put a wire fence around, and that he'd draped with Shoo—rope soaked with creosote, advertised as very effective against dogs, rabbits, and rodents of all kinds. And as for the punishment the young rabbit had taken from whatever it was, he had once seen a mother squirrel get tough with a little one that had strayed from the family tree.

"Would she hurt the young rabbit?" said the younger girl.

"She might. A little."

"This one was hurt a lot," said the eyewitness. She spoke with authority.

"Maybe it was a cat," he said, rallying. "You say it was about the same size."

The children didn't reply. It seemed to him that they did not trust him. His mama-rabbit theory was too good to be true. They believed in the weasel.

"A weasel would've killed it," he said.

"But if he saw *me*?"

"*Did* he see you?"

"Of course."

"Did you see *him*?"

"Of course!" cried the child, impatient with the question. She didn't appear to realize that she was cornered, that having seen the attacker she should be able to describe it. But she was under no obligation to be logical. He decided to wait a few years.

Out in the yard he scrutinized the ground around the playhouse for blood and fur, and saw none. He stepped to the edge of the lilies. Each year the lilies were thicker and less fruitful of flowers, and a gardener would have thinned them out. A gardener, though, would have spoiled this yard—for the fairies who, the children told him, played there. He didn't enter the lilies because he didn't want to encounter what he might.

Passing through the kitchen, he noticed that the children were cutting up a catalogue, both pasting. Apparently the older one could no longer get the younger one to do all the scissor work. "How's the bird?"

"We don't know."

He stopped and got them in focus. "Why don't you know?"

"We haven't looked at it."

"Haven't looked at it! Why haven't you?"

"We've been doing this."

"This is why."

It was a mystery to him how, after crooning over the helpless creature, after entangling him in its fate, they could be this way. This was not the first time, either. "Well, get out there and look at it!"

On the way out to look at it himself, he met them coming back. "He's all right," the older one said grumpily.

"Looks the same, huh?" He didn't catch what they said in reply, which wasn't much anyway. He found the bird where he'd last seen it, beside the back porch. He had expected it to be dying by now. Its ribs showed clearly when it breathed, which was alarming, but he remembered that this had worried him when he first saw the bird. It did seem to be about the same.

He passed through the kitchen and, seeing the children all settled down again, he said, "Find a better place for it. It'll soon be in the sun."

A few moments later, he was intervening. They had the whole yard and yet they were arguing over two patches of shade, neither of which would be good for more than a few minutes. He carried the dishpan out into the yard, and was annoyed that they weren't following him, for he wanted them to see what he was doing and why. He put the dishpan down where the sun wouldn't appear again until morning. He picked it up again. He carried it across the yard to the foot of the white oak. On the ground, directly below the nest, there was and would be sun until evening, but near the trunk there would be shade until morning.

The bird was breathing heavily, as before, but it was in no distress—unless this was distress. He thought not. If the bird had a full coat of feathers, its breathing wouldn't be so noticeable.

He was pleasantly surprised to see a mature dove high above him. The dove wasn't near the nest, wasn't watching him—was just looking unconcerned in another part of the tree—but it was in the right tree. He tried to attract its attention, making what he considered a gentle bird noise. It flew away, greatly disappointing him.

He knelt and lifted the tin of water to the bird's mouth. This he did with no expectation that it would drink, but it did, it definitely did. The bird kept its bill in the water, waggling it once or twice, spilling some, and raised its head slightly—not as a chicken would. He tried a little bread, unsuccessfully. He tried the water again, and again the bird drank. The bread was refused again and also the water when it was offered the third time. This confirmed him in his belief that the bird had been drinking before. This also proved that the bird was able to make decisions. After two drinks, the bird had said, in effect, no more. It hadn't eaten for some time, but it was evidently still sound in mind and body. It might need only a mother's care to live.

He went into the house. In the next two hours, he came to the window frequently. For a while he tried to believe that there might be maternal action at the foot of the oak while he wasn't watching. He knew better, though. All he could believe was that the mother might be staying away because she regarded the dishpan as a trap—assuming, of course, that she had spotted the baby, and assuming also that she gave a damn, which he doubted.

Before dinner he went out and removed the birdhouse and then the bird from the dishpan, gently tipping it into the grass, not touching it. The nest the children had twined together slid with it, but the bird ended up more off than on the nest. There was plenty of good, growing grass under the dove, however. If, as the children claimed, the bird could move a little and if the mother did locate it, perhaps between them—he credited the baby with some intelligence—they might have enough sense to hide out in the lilies of the valley only a few feet away. There would be days ahead of feeding and growth before the little bird could fly, probably too many days to pass on the ground in the open. Once the mother assumed her responsibility, however, everything would become easier—that is, possible. *He* might even build a nest nearby. (One year there had been a dove's nest in a chokecherry tree, only ten feet off the ground.) Within a few yards of the oak there were aged lilac bushes, almost trees, which would be suitable for a nest. At present, though, with the mother delinquent, the situation was impossible.

He looked up into the trees for her, in vain, and then down at the orphan. It had moved. It had taken up its former position precisely in the center of the little raft of grass the children had made for it, and this was painful to see, this little display of order in a thing so small, so dumb, so sure.

It would not drink. He set the water closer, and the bread, just in case, and carried away the dishpan and the birdhouse. He saw the bowel movement in the bottom of the dishpan as a good omen, but was puzzled by the presence of a tiny dead bug of the beetle family. It could mean that the mother had been in attendance, or it could mean that the bug had simply dropped dead from the spraying, a late casualty.

After dinner, standing on the back porch, he heard a disturbance far out in the yard. Blue jays, and up to no good, he thought, and walked toward the noise. When he reached the farthest corner of the yard, the noise ceased, and began again. He looked into the trees across the alley. Then he saw two catbirds in the honeysuckle bushes only six feet away and realized that he had mistaken their rusty cries for those of blue jays at some distance. The catbirds hopped, scolding, from branch to branch. They moved to the next bush, but not because of him, he thought. It was then that he saw the cat in the lilies. He stamped his foot. The cat, a black-and-white one marked like a Holstein cow, plowed through the lilies and out into the alley where the going was good, and was gone. The catbirds followed, flying low, belling the cat with their cries. In the distance he heard blue jays, themselves marauders, join in, doing their bit to make the cat's position known. High overhead he saw two dopey doves doing absolutely nothing about the cat, heard their little dithering noise, and was disgusted with them. It's a wonder you're not extinct, he thought, gazing up at them. They chose that moment to show him the secret of their success.

He walked the far boundaries of the yard, stopping to gaze back at the old frame house, which was best seen at a distance. He had many pictures of it in his mind, for it changed with the seasons, gradually, and all during the day. The old house always looked good to him: in spring when the locust, plum, lilacs, honeysuckle, caragana, and mock orange bloomed around it; in summer, as it was now, almost buried in green; in autumn when the yard was rolling with nuts, crashing with leaves, and the mountain-ash berries turned red; and in winter when, under snow and icicles, with its tall mullioned windows sparkling, it reminded him of an old-fashioned Christmas card. For a hundred years it had been painted barn or Venetian red, with forest-green trim. In winter there were times when the old house, because of the light, seemed to be bleeding; the red then was profound and alive. Perhaps it knew something, after all, he thought. In January the yellow bulldozers would come for it and the trees. One of the old oaks, one that had appeared to be in excellent health, had recently thrown down half of itself in the night. "Herbal suicide," his wife had said.

Reaching the other far corner of the yard, he stood considering the thick black-walnut tree, which he had once, at about this time of year, thought of girdling with a tin shield to keep off the squirrels. But this would have taken a lot of tin, and equipment he didn't own to trim a neighboring maple and possibly an elm, and so he had decided to share the nuts with the squirrels. This year they could have them all. Few of the birds would be there when it happened, but the squirrels—there were at least a dozen in residence—were in for a terrible shock.

He moved toward the house, on the street side of the yard, on the lookout for beer cans and bottles that the college students from their parked cars tossed into the bushes. He knew, from several years of picking up after them, their favorite brand.

He came within twenty yards of the white oak, and stopped. He didn't want to venture too near in case the mother was engaged in feeding the baby, or was just about to make up her mind to do so. In order to see, however, he would have to be a little closer. He moved toward the white oak in an indirect line, and stopped again. The nest was empty. His first thought was that the bird, sensing the approach of darkness, had wisely retreated into the shelter of the lilies of the valley nearby, and then he remembered the recent disturbance on the other side of the yard. The cat had last been seen at what had appeared a safe distance then. He was looking now for feathers, blood, bones. But he saw no such signs of the bird. Again he considered the possibility that it was hiding in the lilies of the valley. When he recalled the bird sitting in the very center of the nest, it did not seem likely that it would leave, ever—unless persuaded by the mother to do so. But he had no faith in the mother, and instead of searching the lilies, he stood where he was and studied the ground around him in a widening circle. The cat could've carried it off, of course, or—again—the bird could be safe among the lilies.

He hurried to the fallen oak. Seeing the little bird at such a distance from the nest, and not seeing it as he'd expected he would, but entire, he had been deceived. The bird was not moving. It was on its back, not mangled but dead. He noted the slate-black feet. Its head was to one side on the grass. The one eye he could see was closed, and the blood all around it, enamel-bright, gave the impression, surprising to him, that it had poured out like paint. He wouldn't have thought such a little thing would even have blood.

He went for the shovel with which he'd turned up no worms for the bird earlier that day. He came back to the bird by a different route, having passed on the other side of a big tree, and saw the little ring of grass that had been the bird's nest. It now looked like a wreath to him.

He dug a grave within a few feet of the bird. The

ground was mossy there. He simply lifted up a piece of it, tucked in the bird, and dropped the sod down like a cover. He pounded it once with the back side of the shovel, thinking the bird would rest easier there than in most ground.

When he looked up from his work, he saw that he had company: Mr. and Mrs. Hahn, neighbors. He told them what had happened, and could see that Mr. Hahn considered him soft. He remembered that Mr. Hahn, who had an interest such as newspapers seemed to think everybody ought to have in atomic explosions, didn't care to discuss the fallout.

The Hahns walked with him through the yard. They had heard there were no mosquitoes there now.

"Apparently it works," he said.

"The city should spray," said Mrs. Hahn.

"At least the swamps," said Mr. Hahn, who was more conservative.

He said nothing. They were perfectly familiar with his theory: that it was wet enough in the lily beds, in the weeds along the river, for mosquitoes to breed. When he argued that there just weren't enough swamps to breed that many mosquitoes, people smiled, and tried to refute his theory—confirmed it—by talking about how little water it took, a birdbath, a tin can somewhere. "In my opinion, they breed right here, in this yard and yours."

"Anyway, they're not here now," said Mrs. Hahn.

He received this not as a compliment but as a polite denial of his theory. They were passing under the mulberry tree. In the bloody atmosphere prevailing in his mind that evening, he naturally thought of the purple grackle that had hung itself from a high branch with a string in the previous summer. "I'm sick of it all."

"Sick of *what*?" said Mrs. Hahn.

The Hahns regarded him as a head case, he knew,

and probably wouldn't be surprised if he said that he
was sick of them. He had stopped trying to adjust his
few convictions and prejudices to company. He just let
them fly. Life was too short. "Insects, birds, and animals
of all kinds," he said. "Nature."

Mr. Hahn smiled. "There'd be too many of those
doves if things like that didn't happen."

"I suppose."

Mr. Hahn said: "Look how the fish live."

He looked at the man with interest. This was the
most remarkable thing Mr. Hahn had ever said in his
presence. But, of course, Mr. Hahn didn't appreciate
the implications. Mr. Hahn didn't see himself in the
picture at all.

"That includes children," he said, pursuing his orig-
inal line. It was the children who were responsible for
bringing the failures of nature to his attention.

Mrs. Hahn, who seemed to feel she was on familiar
ground, gaily laughed. "Everybody who has them com-
plains about them."

"*And* women," he added. He had almost left women
out, and they belonged in. They were responsible for
the children and the success of *Queen for a Day*.

"And men," he added when he caught Mr. Hahn
smiling at the mention of women. Men were at the bottom of it all.

"That doesn't leave much, does it?" said Mr. Hahn.

"No." Who *was* left? God. It wasn't surprising, for
all problems were at bottom theological. He'd like to
put a few questions to God. God, though, knowing his
thoughts, knew his questions, and the world was already in possession of all the answers that would be
forthcoming from God. Compassion for the Holy Family fleeing from Herod was laudable and meritorious,
but it was wasted on soulless rabbits fleeing from soulless weasels. Nevertheless it was there just the same, or

something very like it. As he'd said in the beginning, he was sick of it all.

"There he is now!" cried Mrs. Hahn.

He saw the black-and-white cat pause under the fallen oak.

"Should I get my gun?" said Mr. Hahn.

"No. It's his nature." He stamped his foot and hissed. The cat ran out of the yard. Where were the birds? They could be keeping an eye on the cat. Somewhere along the line they must have said the hell with it. He supposed there was a lesson in that for him. A man couldn't commiserate with life to the full extent of his instincts and opportunities. A man had to accept his God-given limitations.

He accompanied the Hahns around to the front of the house, and there they met a middle-aged woman coming up the walk. He didn't know her, but the Hahns did, and introduced her. Mrs. Snyder.

"It's about civil defense," she said. Every occupant of every house was soon to be registered for the purposes of identification in case of an emergency. Each block would have its warden, and Mrs. Snyder thought that he, since he lived on this property, which took up so much of the block . . .

"No."

"No?"

"No." He couldn't think of a job for which he was less suited, in view of his general outlook. He wouldn't be here anyway. Nor would this house, these trees.

While Mr. and Mrs. Hahn explained to Mrs. Snyder that the place was to become a parking lot for the college, he stood by in silence. He had never heard it explained so well. His friends had been shocked at the idea of doing away with the old house and trees—and for a parking lot!—and although he appreciated their concern, there was nothing to be done, and after a time he was unable to sympathize with them. This they didn't readily understand. It was as if some venerable figure in the community, only known to them but near and dear to him, had been murdered, and he failed to show proper sorrow and anger. The Hahns, however, were explaining how it was, turning this way and that, pointing to this building and that, to sites already taken, to those to be taken soon or in time. For them the words "the state" and "expansion" seemed sufficient. And the Hahns weren't employed by the college and they weren't old grads. It was impossible to account in such an easy way for their enthusiasm. They were scheduled for eviction themselves, they said, in a few years.

When they were all through explaining, it must have been annoying to them to hear Mrs. Snyder's comment. "Too bad," she said. She glanced up at the old red house and then across the street at the new dormitory going up. There had been a parking lot there for a few years, but before that another big old house and trees. The new dormitory, apricot bricks and aluminum windows, was in the same style as the new library, a style known to him and his wife as Blank. "Too bad," Mrs. Snyder said again, with an uneasy look across the street, and then at him.

"There's no defense against that *either*," he said, and if Mrs. Snyder understood what he meant, she didn't show it.

"Well," she said to Mr. Hahn, "how about you?"

They left him then. He put the shovel away, and walked the boundaries of the yard for the last time that day, pausing twice to consider the house in the light of the moment. When he came to the grave, he stopped

and looked around for a large stone. He took one from
the mound where the hydrant was, the only place
where the wild ginger grew, and set it on the grave, not
as a marker but as an obstacle to the cat if it returned,
as he imagined it would. It was getting dark in the yard,
the night coming sooner there because of the great
trees. Now the bats and owls would get to work, he
thought, and went into the doomed house.

BILL

In January, Joe, who had the habit of gambling with himself, made it two to one against his getting a curate that year. Then, early in May, the Archbishop came out to see the new rectory and, in the office area, which was in the basement but surprisingly bright and airy, paused before the doors "PASTOR" and "ASSISTANT" and said, "You're mighty sure of yourself, Father."

"I can dream, can't I, Your Excellency?"

The subject didn't come up again during the visit, and the Archbishop declined Joe's offer of a drink, which may or may not have been significant—hard to say how much the Arch knew about a man—but after he'd departed Joe made it seven to five, trusting his instinct.

Two weeks later, on the eve of the annual shape-up, trusting his instinct again though he'd heard nothing, Joe made it even money.

The next morning, the Chancery (Toohey) phoned to say that Joe had a curate: "Letter follows."

"Wait a minute. Who?"

"He'll be in touch with you." And Toohey hung up.

Maybe it hadn't been decided who would be sent out to Joe's (Church of SS. Francis and Clare, Inglenook), but probably it had, and Toohey just didn't want to say because Joe had asked. That was how Toohey, too long at the Chancery, played the game. Joe didn't think any more about it then.

He grabbed a scratch pad, rushed upstairs to the room, now bare, that would be occupied by his curate (who?), and made a list, which was his response to problems, temporal and spiritual, that required thought.

That afternoon, he visited a number of furniture stores in Inglenook, in Silverstream, the next suburb, and in the city. "Just looking," he said to clerks. After a couple of hours, he had a pretty good idea of the market, but he was unable to act, and then he had to suspend operations in order to beat the rush-hour traffic home.

Afterward, though, he discovered what was wrong. It was his list. Programed without reference to the *relative* importance of the items on it, his list, instead of helping, had hindered him, had caused him to mess around looking at lamps, rugs, and ashtrays. It hadn't told him that everything in the room would be determined, dictated, by the bed. Why bed? Because the room was a *bed-room*. Find the bed, the right bed, and the rest would follow. He knew where he was now, and he was glad that time had run out that afternoon. Toward the last, he had been suffering from shopper's fatigue, or he wouldn't have considered that knotty-pine suite, with its horseshoe brands and leather thongs, simply because it had a clean, masculine look that bedroom furniture on the whole seemed to lack.

That evening, he sat down in the quiet of his study, in his Barcalounger chair, with some brochures and a drink, and made another list. This one was different and should have been easy for him—with office equipment he really knew where he was, and probably no priest in the diocese knew so well—but for that very reason he couldn't bring himself to furnish the curate's office as other pastors would have done, as, in fact, he had planned to do. Why spoil a fine office by installing inferior, economy-type equipment? Why not move the pastor's desk and typewriter, both recent purchases, into the curate's office? Why not get the pastor one of those laminated mahogany desks, maybe Model DK 100, sleek and contemporary but warm and friendly as only wood can be? (The pastor was tired of his unfriendly metal desk and his orthopedic chair.) Why not get the pastor a typewriter with different type? (What, *again*? Yes, because he was tired of that phony script.) But keep the couch and chairs in the pastor's office, and let the new chairs—two or three, and no couch—go straight into the curate's office.

The next morning, he drove to the city with the traffic, and swiftly negotiated the items on his office list, including a desk, Model DK 100, and a typewriter with different type, called "editorial," and said to be used by newscasters.

"Always a pleasure to do business with you, Father," the clerk said.

The scene then changed to the fifth floor of a large department store, which Joe had visited the day before, and there life got difficult again. What had brought him back was a fourposter bed with pineapple finials. The clerk came on a little too strong.

"The double bed's making a big comeback, Father."

"That so?"

"What I'd have, if I had the choice."

"Yes, well." Joe liked the bed, especially the pineapples, but he just couldn't see the curate (who?) in it. Get it for himself, then, and give the curate the pastor's bed—*it* was a single. And then what? The pastor's bed, of unfriendly metal and painted like a car, hospital grey, would dictate nothing about the other things for the room. Besides, it wouldn't be fair to the curate, would it?

"Lot of bed for the money, Father."

"Too much bed."

The clerk then brought out some brochures and binders with colored tabs. So Joe sat down with him on a bamboo chaise longue, and, passing the literature back and forth between them, they went to work on Joe's problem. They discovered that Joe could order the traditional type of bed in a single, in several models— cannonballs, spears, spools (Jenny Lind)—but not pineapples, which, it seemed, had been discontinued by the maker. "But I wonder about that, Father. Tell you what. With your permission, I'll call North Carolina."

Joe let him go ahead, after more discussion, mostly about air freight, but when the clerk returned to the chaise longue he was shaking his head. North Carolina had gone to lunch. North Carolina would call back, though, in an hour or so, after checking the warehouse. "You wouldn't take cannonballs or spears, Father? Or Jenny Lind?"

"Not Jenny Lind."

"You like cannonballs, Father?"

"Yes, but I prefer the other."

"Pineapples."

Since nothing could be done about the other items on his list until he found out about the bed—or beds, for he had decided to order two beds, singles, with matching chests, plus box springs and mattresses, eight pieces in all—Joe went home to await developments.

At six minutes to three, the phone rang. "St. Francis," Joe said.

"Earl, Father."

"*Earl?*"

"At the store, Father."

"Oh, hello, Earl."

Earl said that North Carolina *could* supply, and would air-freight to the customer's own address. So beds and chests would arrive in a couple of days, Friday at the outside, and box springs and mattresses, these from stock, would be on the store's Thursday delivery to Inglenook.

"O.K., Father?"

"O.K., Earl."

Joe didn't try to do any more that day.

The next morning, he took delivery of the office equipment (which Mrs. P.—Mrs. Pelissier—the housekeeper, must have noticed), and so he got a late start on his shopping. He began where he'd left off the day before. Earl, spotting him among the lamps, came over to say hello. When he saw Joe's list, he recommended the store's interior-decorating department—"Mrs. Fox, if she's not out on a job." With Joe's permission, Earl went to a phone, and Mrs. Fox soon appeared among the lamps. Slightly embarrassed, Joe told her what he thought—that the room ought to be planned around the bed, since it was a *bed*room. Mrs. Fox smacked her lips and shrieked (to Earl), "*He* doesn't need *me!*"

As a matter of fact, Mrs. Fox proved very helpful—steered Joe from department to department, protected him from clerks, took him into stockrooms and onto a freight elevator, and remembered curtains and bedspreads (Joe bought two), which weren't on his list but were definitely needed. Finally, Mrs. Fox had the easy chair and other things brought down to the parking lot and put into his car. These could have gone out on the Thursday delivery, but Joe wanted to see how the room would look even without the big stuff—the bed, the chest, the student's table, and the revolving bookcase. Mrs. Fox felt the same way. Twice in the store she'd expressed a desire to see the room, and he'd managed to change the subject, and then she did it again, in the parking lot—was *dying* to see the room, she shrieked, just as he was driving away. He just smiled. What else could he do? He couldn't have Mrs. Fox coming out there.

In some ways, things were moving too fast. He still hadn't told Mrs. P. that he was getting a curate—hadn't because he was afraid if he did, she'd ask, as he had, "Who?" Who, indeed? He still didn't know, and the fact that he didn't would, if admitted, make him look foolish in Mrs. P.'s eyes. It would also put the Church—administrationwise—in a poor light.

That evening, after Mrs. P. had gone home, Joe unloaded the car, which he'd run into the garage because the easy chair was clearly visible in the trunk. It took him four trips to get all his purchases up to the room. Then, using a kitchen chair, listening to the ball game and drinking beer, he put up the curtain rods. (The janitor, if asked to, would wonder why, and if told, would tell Mrs. P., who would ask, "Who?") When Joe had the curtains up, tiebacks and all, he took a much needed bath, changed, and made himself a gin-and-tonic. He carried it into the room, dark now—he had been waiting for this moment—and turned on the lamps he'd bought. O.K.—and when the student's table came, the student's lamp, now on the little bedside table, would look even better. He had chosen one with a yellow shade, rather than green, so the room would appear cheerful, and it certainly did. He tried the easy chair, the matching footstool, the gin-and-tonic. O.K. He sat there for some time, one foot going to sleep on the rose-and-blue hooked rug while he wondered why— why he hadn't heard anything from the curate.

The next day, Thursday, he gave Mrs. P. the afternoon off, saying he planned to eat out that evening, and so she wasn't present when the box springs, mattresses, student's table and revolving bookcase came, at twenty after four—the hottest time of day. He had a lot of trouble with the mattresses—really a job for two strong men, one to pull on the mattress, one to hold on to the carton—and had to drink two bottles of beer to restore his body salts. He took a much needed bath, changed, and, feeling too tired to go out, made himself some ham sandwiches and a gin-and-tonic. He used a whole lime —it was his salad—and ate in his study while watching the news: people starving in Asia and Mississippi. He went without dessert. Suddenly, he jumped up and got busy around the place, did the dishes—dish—and locked the church. When darkness came, he was back where he'd been the night before—in the room, in the chair, with a glass, wondering why he hadn't heard anything from the curate.

It was customary for the newly ordained men to take a few days off to visit and shake down their friends and relatives. Ordinations, though, had been held on Saturday. It was now Thursday, almost Friday, and still no word. What to do? He had called people at the seminary, hoping to learn the curate's name and perhaps something of his character, just in the course of conversation. ("Understand you're getting So-and-So, Joe.") But it hadn't happened—everybody he asked to speak to (the entire faculty, it seemed) had left for vacationland. He had then called the diocesan paper and, with pencil ready, asked for a complete rundown on the new appointments, but the list hadn't come over from the Chancery yet. ("They can be pretty slow over there, Father." "Toohey, you mean?" "Monsignor's pretty busy, Father, and we don't push him on a thing like this—it's not what we call hard news.")

So, really, there was nothing to do, short of calling the Chancery. Early in the week, it might have been done—that was when Joe made his mistake—but it was out of the question now. He didn't want to expose the curate to censure and run the risk of turning him against his pastor, and he also didn't want the Chancery to know what the situation was at SS. Francis and Clare's, one of the best-run parishes in the diocese, though it certainly wasn't his fault. It was the curate's fault, it was Toohey's fault. "Letter follows." If called on that, Toohey would say, "Didn't say when. Busy here," and hang up. That was how Toohey played the game. Once, when Joe had called for help and said he'd die if he didn't get away for a couple of weeks, Toohey had said, "Die," and hung up. Rough. If the Church ever got straightened out administrationwise, Toohey and his kind would have to go, but that was one of those long-term objectives. In the meantime, Joe and his kind would have to soldier on, and Joe would. It was hard, though, after years of waiting for a curate, after finally getting one, not to be able to mention it. While shopping, Joe had run into two pastors who would have been interested to hear of his good fortune, and one had even raised the subject of curates, had said that he was getting a *change*, "Thank God!" Joe hadn't thought much about it then—the "Thank God!" part—but now he did, and, swallowing the weak last inch of his drink, came face to face with the ice.

What, he thought—what if the curate, the unknown curate, *wasn't* one of the newly ordained men? What if he was one of those bad-news guys? A young man with five or six parishes behind him? Or a man as old as himself, or older, a retread, a problem priest? Or a gold-brick who figured, since he was paid by the month, he wouldn't report until the first, Sunday? Or a slob who wouldn't take care of the room? These were sobering thoughts to Joe. He got up and made another drink.

The next morning, when he returned from a trip to the dump, where he personally disposed of his empties, Mrs. P. met him at the door. "Somebody who says he's your assistant—"

"Yes, yes. Where is he?"

"Phoned. Said he'd be here tomorrow."

"*Tomorrow?*" But he didn't want Mrs. P. to get the idea that he was disappointed, or that he didn't know what was going on. "Good. Did he say what time?"

"He just asked about confessions."

"So he'll be here in time for confessions. Good."

"Said he was calling from Whipple."

"*Whipple?*"

"Said he was down there buying a car."

Joe nodded, as though he regarded Whipple, which he'd driven through one or twice, as an excellent place to buy a car. He was waiting for Mrs. P. to continue.

"That's all *I* know," she said, and shot off to the kitchen. Hurt. Not his fault. Toohey's fault. Curate's fault. Not telling her about the curate was bad, but doing it as he would have had to would have been worse. Better she think less of him than know the truth

—and think less of the Church. He took the sins of
curates and administrators upon him.

That afternoon, he waited until four o'clock before
he got on the phone to Earl. "Say, what is this? I
thought you said Friday at the outside."

"Oh, oh," said Earl, and didn't have to be told who
was calling, or about what. He said he'd put a tracer on
the order, and promised to call back right away, which
he did. "Hey, Father, guess what? The order's at our
warehouse. North Carolina goofed."

"That so?" said Joe, but he wasn't interested in Earl's
analysis of North Carolina's failure to ship to customer's
own address, and cut in on it. He described his bed
situation, as he hadn't before for Earl, in depth. He was
going to be short a bed—no, not that night but the next,
when his assistant would be there, and also a monk of
advanced age who helped out on weekends and slept in
the guest room. No, the bed in the guest room, to answer Earl's question, was a single—actually, a cot. Yes,
Joe could put his assistant on the box spring and mattress, but wouldn't like to do it, and didn't see why he
should. He'd been promised delivery by Friday at the
outside. He didn't care if Inglenook *was* in Monday and
Thursday territory. In the end, he was promised delivery the next day, Saturday.

"O.K., Father?"

"O.K., Earl."

The next afternoon, a panel truck, scarred and bearing
no name, pulled up in front of the rectory at seven minutes after four. Joe didn't know what to make of it. He
stayed inside the rectory until the driver and his helper
unloaded a carton, then rushed out, and was about to
ask them to unload at the back door and save them-

selves a few steps when a word on the carton stopped him. "Hold everything!" And it wasn't, as he'd hoped, simply a matter of a word on a carton. Oh, no. On investigation, the beds proved to be as described on their cartons—cannonballs. "Hold everything. I have to call the store."

On the way to the telephone, passing Father Otto, the monk of advanced age, who was another who hadn't been told about the curate, and now appeared curious to know what was happening in the street, Joe wished that monks were forbidden to wear their habits away from the monastery. Flowing robes, Joe felt, had a bad effect on his parishioners, made him, in his cassock, look second-best in their eyes, and also reminded non-Catholics of the Reformation.

"Say, what is this?" he said, on the phone.

"Oh, oh," said Earl when he learned what had happened. "North Carolina goofed."

"Now, *look*," said Joe, and really opened up on Earl and the store. "I don't like the way you people do business," he said, pausing to breathe.

"Correct me if I'm wrong, Father, but didn't you say you liked cannonballs?"

"Better than Jenny Lind, I said. But that's not the point. I prefer the other, and that's what I said. You know what 'prefer' means, don't you?"

"Pineapples."

"You've got me over a barrel, Earl."

In the end, despite what he'd indicated earlier, Joe said he'd take delivery. "But we're through," he told Earl, and hung up.

He returned to the street where, parked behind the panel truck, there was now a new VW beetle, and there, it seemed, standing by the opened cartons with Father Otto, the driver, and his helper, was Joe's curate—big and young, obviously one of the newly ordained men.

Seeing Joe, he left the others and came smiling toward
him.

"Where you been?" Joe said—like an old pastor, he
thought.

The curate stopped smiling. "Whipple."

Joe put it another way. "Why didn't you give me a
call?"

"I did."

"Before yesterday?"

"I did. Don't know how many times I called. You
were never in."

"Didn't know what to think," Joe said, ignoring the
curate's point like an old pastor, and, looking away,
wished that the beetle—light brown, or dark yellow,
sort of a caramel—was another color, and also that it
wasn't parked where it was, adding to the confusion.
(The driver's helper was showing Father Otto how his
dolly worked.) "Could've left your name with the
housekeeper."

"I kept thinking I'd get you if I called again. You
were never in."

Joe moved toward the street, saying, "Yes, well, I've
been out a lot lately. Could've left your name, Father."

"I did, Father. Yesterday."

"Yes, well." Standing by the little car, viewing the
books and luggage inside, Joe wished that he could start
over, that he hadn't started off as he had. He had meant
to welcome the curate. It wasn't his fault that he hadn't
—look at the days and nights of needless anxiety, and
look what time it was now—but still he wanted to make
up for it. "Better drive your little car around to the
back, Father, and unload," he said. "The housekeeper'll
show you the room. Won't ask you to hear confessions
this afternoon." And, having opened the door of the
little car for the curate, he closed it for him, saying,
through the window, "See you later, Father."

When he straightened up, he saw that Big Mouth, a neighbor and a parishioner, had arrived to inspect the cartons, heard him questioning Father Otto, saw, too, that Mrs. P. had decided to sweep the front walk and was working that way. Joe called to her.

"I've bought a few things—besides the bed and chest here—for the curate's room," he told her, so she wouldn't be too surprised when she saw them. Then he gave her the key to the room, saying, perhaps needlessly, that she'd find it locked, and that the box springs, mattresses, and bedspreads would be found within. The other bed—the one that should and would have been his but for the interest shown in it by Father Otto and Big Mouth—the other bed and chest, he told Mrs. P., should go into the guest room. "Fold up the cot and put it somewhere. Get the curate to help you—he's not hearing this afternoon."

Turning then to the little group around the cartons, he saw that his instructions to Mrs. P. had been overheard and understood. The little group—held together by the question "Would he take delivery?"—was breaking up. He thanked the driver and his helper for waiting, nodded to Big Mouth, said "Coming?" to Father Otto, since it was now time for confessions, and walked toward the church. He took the sins of curates and administrators and North Carolina upon him. He gave another his bed.

That evening, after confessions, and after Father Otto had retired to the new bed in the guest room, Joe and the curate sat on in the pastor's study. Joe, doing most of the talking, had had less than usual, the curate more, it seemed—he was yawning. "Used to be," Joe was saying, "we all drove black cars. I still do." Joe, while he didn't want to hurt the curate's feelings, just couldn't understand why a priest, even a young priest today, able to buy a new car should pick one the color of the curate's. "Maybe it's not important."

"Think I'll turn in, Father."

Joe hated to go to bed, and changed the subject slightly. "How's the room? O.K.?"

"O.K."

Joe had been expecting a bit more. Had he hurt the curate's feelings? "It's not important, what I was saying."

The curate smiled. "My uncle's the dealer in Whipple. He gave me a good deal on the car, but that was part of it—the color."

"I see." Joe tried not to appear as interested as he suddenly was. "What's he call his place—Whipple Volkswagen? I know a lot of 'em do. That's what they call it here—Inglenook Volkswagen."

"He calls it by his own name."

"I see. And this is your father's brother?"

"My mother's."

"I see."

"Think I'll turn in now, Father."

"Yeah. Maybe we should. Sunday's always a tough day."

The next morning, with Joe watching from the sacristy, and later from the rear of the church, the curate said his first Mass in the parish. He was slow, of course, but he wasn't fancy, and he didn't fall down. His sermon was standard, marred only by his gestures (once or twice he looked like a bad job of dubbing), and he read the announcements well. He neglected to introduce himself to the congregation, but that might be done the following week in the parish bulletin.

The day began to go wrong, though, when, after his

second Mass, the curate mentioned an invitation he had
to dine out with a classmate. "Well, all right," Joe said,
writing off the afternoon but not the evening.

He still hadn't written off the evening, entirely, at
eighteen after eleven. The door of the pastor's study
was open, and the pastor was clearly visible in his
Barcalounger chair, having a nightcap, but the curate
went straight to his room, and could soon be heard running a bath.

So Joe, despite the change from a week ago, had
spent Sunday as usual—the afternoon with the papers,
TV, a nap, and Father Otto (until it was time for his
bus), and the evening alone. Most of it. At seven-thirty,
he'd had a surprise visit from Earl, his wife, and two of
their children.

The next morning, Joe laid an unimportant letter on
the curate's metal desk. "Answer this, will you? I've
made some notes on the margin so you'll know what to
say. Keep it brief. Sign *your* name—Assistant Pastor.
But let me have a look at it before you seal it." And that,
he thought, is that.

"Does it have to be *typed*?"

"What d'ya mean?"

"Can't *type* it."

"What d'ya mean?"

"Can't *type*."

Joe just stood there in a distressed state. "Can't
type," he said. "You mean at the sem you did everything
in longhand? Term papers and everything?"

The curate, who seemed to think that too much was
being made of his disability, nodded.

"Hard to believe," Joe said. "Why, you must've been
the only guy in your class not to use a typewriter."

"There was one other guy."

Joe was somewhat relieved—at least the gambler in
him was—to know that he hadn't been quite as unlucky

as he'd supposed. "But you must've heard guys all around you using typewriters. Didn't you ever wonder why?"

"I never owned a typewriter. Never saw the need." The curate sounded proud, like somebody who brushes his teeth with table salt. "I write a good, clear hand."

Joe snorted. "*I* write a good, clear hand. But I don't do my parish correspondence by hand. And I hope *you* won't when you're a pastor."

"The hell with it, then."

Joe, who had been walking around in a distressed state, stopped and looked at the curate, but the curate —pretty clever—wouldn't look back. He was getting out a cigarette. Joe shook his head, and walked around shaking it. "Father, Father," he said.

"Father, hell," said the curate, emitting smoke. "You should've put in for a stenographer, not a priest."

Joe stopped, stood still, and sniffed. "Great," he said, nodding his head. "Sounds great, Father. But what does it *mean*? Does it mean you expect me to do the lion's share of the donkey work around here? While you're out saving souls? Or sitting up in your room? Does it mean when you're a pastor you'll expect your curate to do what you never had to do? I hope not, Father. Because, you know, Father, when you're a pastor it may be years before you have a curate. You may never have one, Father. You may end up in a one-horse parish. Lots of guys do. You won't be able to afford a secretary, or public stenographers, and you won't care to trust your correspondence to nuns, to parishioners. You'll never be your own man. You'll always be an embarrassment to yourself and others. Let's face it, Father. Today, a man who can't use a typewriter is as ill-equipped for parish life as a man who can't drive a car. Go ahead. Laugh. Sneer. But it's true. You don't want to be like Toohey, do you? *He* can't type, and he's set this diocese back a hundred years. He writes 'No can do' on everything and returns it to the sender. For official business he uses scratch paper put out by the Universal Portland Cement Company."

Depressed by the thought of Toohey and annoyed by the curate's cool, if that was what it was, Joe retired to his office. He sat down at his new desk and made a list. Presently, he appeared in the doorway between the offices, wearing his hat. "And, Father," he continued, "when you're a pastor, what if you get a curate like yourself? Think it over. I have to go out now. Mind the store."

Joe drove to the city and bought a typing course consisting of a manual and phonograph records, and he also bought the bed—it was still there—the double, with pineapples. He was told that if he ever wished to order a matching chest or dresser there would be no trouble at all, and that the bed, along with box spring and mattress, would be on the Thursday delivery to Inglenook.

"O.K., Father?"

"O.K., Earl."

And that afternoon Joe, in his office, had a phone call from Mrs. Fox. She just wondered if everything was O.K., she said—as if she didn't know. She was still dying to see the room. "What's it *like!*" Joe said he thought the room had turned out pretty well, thanked Mrs. Fox for helping him, and also for calling, and hung up.

Immediately, the phone rang again. "St. Francis," Joe said.

"Bill there?"

"*Bill?*"

"For *me?*" said the curate, who had been typing away, or, anyway, typing.

Joe tried to look right through the wall. (The door

between the offices was open, but the angle was wrong.) "Take it over there," he said, and switched the call.

There were no further developments that day.

None the next day.

And none the next.

No more phone calls for the curate, and no mail addressed to him, and nothing in the diocesan paper, and no word from Toohey. And Mrs. P. with her "he" and "him" was no help, nor was the janitor with his "young Father," and Father Otto wouldn't be there until Saturday. But in one way or another, sooner or later, perhaps in time for the next parish bulletin, though the odds were now against that, Joe hoped to learn Bill's last name.

FOLKS

Some time later when Jean and I had both gotten married and our husbands had been brought into our very close relationship, we disclosed our early experiences one night. When our husbands first heard our story, they were not only shocked but disbelieving. However, they believed readily when Jean went over and sat on my husband's lap while I beckoned her husband into the other room. Since then we have swapped regularly and have recently added two more couples. We are all very close friends so have no special rules. All four couples met recently in a big cabin in the mountains and it worked so successfully that we plan to try it for a full week next summer.*

* From *Mr.*, Vol. 4, No. 6, whose editors say: "Any assumption that we, because we have had the courage to present a factual and

Dear Lloyd and Jean:

I am doing my Xmas letters, and Les says not to forget you folks, and so here I come. It's almost a year since you moved away, and all I can say is we sure do miss you both. I wish you could see our tree. Les got it from the same guy down at the plant. We added more lights and now have 128. The whole block agreed not to have roof displays this year. Lloyd's bad fall last year had a lot to do with this decision. Only Bensons held out. They would. They have a new Snow White but the same old dwarfs. He came to Les about using ours, said since we wouldn't be needing them this year. Of course Les had to turn him down. We were all worried about the couple that moved into your house, since he is an electrician, but they promised they wouldn't have a roof display. Now it looks like they won't even have a tree. She works, I guess. Both of them nice-looking, but Les thinks they don't get along. They sure keep to themselves.

   Say, we were sorry not to see you at Rocky Ridge last summer, but didn't expect you when you didn't write. I remember Lloyd said he might have to take his vacation at a different time. Was that it? Well, after two days of pouring rain, we decided to drive up to Yellowstone. Just the two of us. Some drive, but this new wagon we have can really eat up the road. Came back through the Black Hills. They needed rain. I suppose you got the cards.

   Say, the big tube burned out about ten days ago. Didn't you say it was almost practically new? The serviceman (Red) tried to tell me it came with the set. Did you ever find the warranty papers? Les wanted to

---

unemotional report, therefore sympathize with the points of view described is a complete misreading of our purpose."

wait until we could afford color, but I didn't think it would be fair to him, with the Bowl games coming up, and so we now have a new picture tube. How many channels where you are now?

Les is giving me a gift certificate that I may apply on a dryer. It is now definite we are getting natural gas in the spring. Do you have it there? He is getting an outboard motor from me. He says what should we do with that old kicker you forgot and left in our garage. Be glad to send it to you. Or if you want us to try and sell it for you, we will. Just let us know. By the way, what do you think we should do about the power mower? If you want to keep it, that's O.K. with us. Or if you want to send it to us, that's O.K., too. In that case, we would forward you your share in it ($44). Maybe you could let us know your decision when you write about the old outboard motor? Lloyd, will you get Jean to write? Les says he's never heard of people like you folks for not writing, and I agree. Ha. Ha.

Hey, don't get us wrong about the mower. If you want us to have it, we will forward you your share ($44) right away, but we don't expect you to send it back unless you want to. Les says you might be smart to hold on to it, and not have to go to the trouble and expense of sending it back. Whatever you decide to do is O.K.

Les is talking about bed and so I'll close with a Merry Xmas and a Happy New Year. Hope our card arrived safely. Yours hasn't come as yet. As always,

Les and Lil

P.S. Les just called about the freight charges in case you decide to send it back. $5 or $6. You don't have to crate it. We don't want to tell you what to do, but it looks like you'd be smart to just forward our share

($44). We used Bensons' last summer, but we hated to ask for it, and the grass got so long each time. Don't want to go through that again and would appreciate hearing from you soon so we can make our plans for the coming year. Les says if you want to send it back we'll split the freight with you—and of course forward you your full share ($44).

KEYSTONE

At his desk in the Chancery, the brownstone mansion that was also his residence, John Dullinger, Bishop of Ostergothenburg (Minnesota), was hard at work on a pastoral letter, this one to be read from the pulpits of the diocese in some five weeks. The Bishop was about to mention the keystone of authority, as he did so often in his pastoral letters, that stone without which . . . when Monsignor Holstein, Vicar-General of the diocese and rector of the Cathedral, a lanky man in his late sixties, arrived with the Minneapolis *Tribune* and a paper bag. *"Wie geht's?"* said Monsignor Holstein, and deposited the bag on the desk.

The Bishop peeked into the bag, said "Oh," and,

with a nod, thanked Monsignor Holstein for his kindness —for the fine new appointment book. It was that time of year again.

"I hear Scuza's worse, John," said Monsignor Holstein.

The Bishop had heard this, too, but assumed that Monsignor Holstein had later word. New Pilsen, where Father Scuza lay dying, was Monsignor Holstein's hometown.

"A bad month, John."

The Bishop sighed. He figured to lose a couple of men every December, and had already lost one that year.

"Another foreign movie coming to the Orpheum, but I can't find out much about it—only that it's Italian," said Monsignor Holstein.

The Bishop sighed.

Monsignor Holstein, who had rolled up the Minneapolis *Tribune*, whacked himself across the hand with it, but did not sit down. On mornings when there was clear and present danger in the diocese—a dance for ninth-graders scheduled for the Eagles' Hall, *Martin Luther* coming to the Orpheum—Monsignor Holstein sat down and beat himself about his black shoes and white socks with the Minneapolis *Tribune*, while the Bishop, a stocky man, opened and shut his mouth like a fish, and said, "Brrr-jorrk-brrrr." On such mornings, by the time the Bishop got the paper it was in poor shape, and so was he. But this wasn't going to be one of those mornings. Monsignor Holstein was about to depart.

"Like me to take that over to the printer?" he asked, looking down at the pastoral letter.

"Not finished."

When Monsignor Holstein was halfway to the door, he saw that he had the paper in his hand, and came back to deliver it. "Like me to wait a few minutes?"

"*No.*" There was more to writing a pastoral letter than getting it to the printer—a lot more than Monsignor Holstein would ever know. He'd never make a bishop.

"Hello, Tootsie," said Monsignor Holstein when he opened the door, addressing the housekeeper's kitten, whose name was not Tootsie but Tessie—and the Bishop wished the man would remember that. "*Raus,* Tootsie!"

"It's all right," said the Bishop, and the kitten came over Monsignor Holstein's shoe, kicking up her heels.

While waiting for the kitten to come and sit on his lap—Monsignor Holstein had upset Tessie—the Bishop checked the helpful data in the new appointment book, as was his custom each year. He was sorry to see that the approximate transit time from New York to Minneapolis by air was still given as seven hours, which took no account of jet travel, and that among the cities with population over fifty thousand there were more places than ever that he hadn't heard of, most of them in California, and that Fargo, North Dakota, which he regarded as his hometown, though he'd been brought up on a farm near there, was still not listed. Perhaps next year. He saw that young Kennedy was now among the Presidents—the youngest ever, except Theodore Roosevelt, to hold that high office—but that Alaska and Hawaii were not among the states. Otherwise—postage rates, stains and how to remove them, points of Constitutional law, weights and measures, weather wisdom, and so on—everything was the same as in the previous edition, including nicknames of the states and the state flowers (Alaska and Hawaii missing). Then, as was his custom, the Bishop examined his conscience:

Good Rules for Businessmen
Don't worry, don't overbuy; don't go security.
Keep your vitality up; keep insured; keep sober; keep cool.

Stick to chosen pursuits, but not to chosen methods.
Be content with small beginnings and develop them.
Be wary of dealing with unsuccessful men.
Be cautious, but when a bargain is made stick to it.
Keep down expenses, but don't be stingy.
Make friends, but not favorites.
Don't take new risks to retrieve old losses.
Stop a bad account at once.
Make plans ahead, but don't make them in cast iron.
Don't tell what you are to do until you have done it.

To the extent that these rules could be made to apply to him—and all of them could, to an extent—the Bishop was doing pretty well, he thought. Presently, with the cat on his lap, he took a call from the editor of the diocesan weekly, Father Rapp, who said that Monsignor Holstein had just left, after giving him an argument over the spelling of "godlessness." "I told him we never capitalize it," Father Rapp said. " 'Then you better begin,' he told me."

"Don't capitalize it," said the Bishop, and returned to the pastoral letter.

Father Gau, the Chancellor, who had put through the call, entered the office, saying, "I thought I'd better let him talk to you."

"Took care of it."

"Is that ready to go over, Your Excellency?"

The Bishop looked down at the pastoral letter. "No —and what's the big hurry?"

"No hurry, Your Excellency." Father Gau smiled in that nice way he had. "I guess I just wanted to read it."

*   *   *

Three days later, the episcopal Cadillac went to New Pilsen for Father Scuza's funeral. Father Gau was at the wheel, the Bishop and Monsignor Holstein in the back seat, where there was some talk, on the Vicar-General's part, of possible successors to the deceased. The Bishop was careful not to commit himself. St. John Nepomuk's, where Father Scuza had been pastor, was one of the most important parishes in the diocese, and the Bishop intended to take more of a hand in such appointments. Every pastor in Ostergothenburg, where there were three churches besides the Cathedral, was one of Monsignor Holstein's men.

After the funeral, on the way back to Ostergothenburg, Monsignor Holstein raised the matter again. "We were down in the church basement, and Leo"—who was Monsignor Holstein's choice for pastor of St. John Nepomuk's—"says why not heat the rectory from the church? Run a pipe underground, and convert the rectory from hot water to steam. Not a bad idea."

The Bishop said nothing.

"I was worried about the radiators in the rectory, but Leo says they're sound. Just have to watch your joints when you go to steam. And switch from oil to gas, Leo says. That's one thing Leo understands—heating."

The Bishop liked Leo well enough. Leo might easily have had the job in days past, but he was one of Monsignor Holstein's men.

"House needs a lot of work," said Monsignor Holstein. "As usual, curates don't give a damn. Saw their rooms—nails in the walls and woodwork, and so on. Whoever goes there will have plenty to do. I'd say Leo's your man, John."

The Bishop said nothing.

As if he'd settled that matter, Monsignor Holstein moved on to the next one. How did the Bishop feel about relocating the big cross in the cemetery so that it would be visible from the new highway? "John, wouldn't it be fine if, next summer, people driving north on their vacations could see the cross?" Then, not mentioning the argument he'd had with Father Rapp, although Father Rapp was present now, riding up in front with Father Gau, Monsignor Holstein got onto the spelling of "godlessness." He said he could see how the word, under special circumstances, might not be capitalized. A heathen of no faith at all—and there were many such in ancient Rome, by all accounts—might be said to be godless as well as Godless. "But, of course, when we use the word, we don't mean anything like that, do we? I don't know whether I make myself clear or not."

Father Gau and Father Rapp, no longer conversing, seemed to be listening for the Bishop's response. It was the Bishop, after all, who had said, "Don't capitalize it." Later, the Bishop had checked the dictionary and found himself right, but as he saw it now the dictionary was wrong. He said nothing.

Father Gau glanced around and, smiling, said, "How would you spell 'atheism,' Monsignor? With a capital 'T'?"

By tradition in the diocese of Ostergothenburg, whoever became chancellor had to be a good, safe driver. Always before, with his long confirmation trips in mind, the Bishop had taken a young man a few years out of the seminary—a practice that might have been criticized more if the diocese hadn't enjoyed the services of a very able, though aging, bishop and a strong vicar-general. For a number of years, Monsignor Holstein had had a lot to say about who should be chancellor, but Father Gau had been the Bishop's own choice for the job. He had come to it at the ripe old age of forty, after years spent entirely in rural parishes, ultimately as pastor in Grasshopper Lake, a little place that hadn't been much in the news until he went there—until, to be more exact, Father Rapp, a classmate of Father Gau's, took over as editor (and photographer) of the diocesan paper.

In May, on a confirmation trip to Grasshopper Lake, the Bishop had had a chance to see some of the wayside shrines he'd been reading about (and seen pictures of). They weren't as close to the road as he would have liked them, but Minnesota wasn't Austria, and the highway department had to have its clearance. The figurines in the shrines were perhaps too much alike, as if from the same hand or mold, and the crosses had been cut from plywood. But, garnished with the honest flowers of the field, as they were in May, these shrines—these outward manifestations of the simple faith of simple people in a wide and wicked world—were a very pretty sight to the Bishop. When he'd pulled up at the church in Grasshopper Lake, little children had suddenly appeared and, grouping themselves around his car, raised their trained voices in song, pure song. The Bishop had never heard the like. "First time I ever heard angels singing, and in German at that!" he told the congregation before beginning what turned out to be a good, long sermon.

Late in August, returning from a trip that had taken him to the northern border of the diocese, the Bishop had paused at Grasshopper Lake. It was the day of the parish's harvest festival. Such occasions still had meaning in the Ostergothenburg diocese, the Bishop believed, and he did all he could to encourage them, only asking that they be brought to a close by sundown, that there be no dancing, and that pastors keep an eye on the beer stand. Father Gau was doing this when the Bishop arrived, and was *not* tending bar, which was something the Bishop didn't want to see, as he'd said time and again. Together they had strolled among the people, the Bishop smiling upon the pies and cakes and upon the women who had baked them, and occasionally giving his hand to a man for shaking. To the grownups he'd say, "You earned this. You worked hard all year," and to the children, "Give us a song!" And, since he was still a long way from home, he had kept moving, in time with the little *Ach-du-lieber-Augustin* band that played in the shade of a big tree, until he was almost back to his car—in which his chancellor of the moment sat listening to the Game of the Day. After asking whether Father Gau's driver's license was in good order, and hearing that it was, the Bishop had said, "Like to live in Ostergothenburg, Father?"

"I'm happy here, Your Excellency."

"I can see that."

"What parish, Your Excellency?"

"I'm looking for a new chancellor."

"Gee," Father Gau had said. "Gee, Your Excellency."

In September, Father Gau had moved into the Cathedral rectory. He handled the routine work at the Chancery, drove the Bishop's car, heard confessions at the Cathedral on Saturdays, and said two Masses there on Sundays. He also organized a children's choir—this at the earnest request of the Bishop. All went well. Then, with the Bishop's consent, Father Gau formed a men's chorus, and there was trouble. Mr. McKee, the director of the Cathedral choir, a mixed group, said that if male members of the choir wanted to get together on purely social occasions and sing "Dry Bones," that was one thing, but if they were going to sing sacred music, that was something else. The men's chorus would be a choir, and a choir couldn't serve two directors, said Mr. McKee and Monsignor Holstein backed him up. Father Gau took no part in the controversy. In fact, he offered to resign as director of the men's chorus, or to disband it, or to turn it over to Mr. McKee—and the children's choir as well, if that would help any. The men of the chorus wouldn't have this, nor would the mothers of the children. The Bishop said nothing—wouldn't discuss the matter with anybody, not even Monsignor Holstein. In the end, in a surprise move, Mr. McKee resigned. And so Father Gau, who already had enough to do, was obliged to assume the direction of the choir. But what the Bishop had feared, an all-out choir war, hadn't happened, and for this he was grateful to all concerned.

Then, a week before Christmas, soon after Father Scuza's funeral, the men of the chorus put on bright tights and sweatshirts and, thus attired, went caroling through the streets of downtown Ostergothenburg. The Ostergothenburg *Times*, whose editor Father Gau had already got to know better than the Bishop ever had (the Bishop didn't like the man's politics), printed a very nice story about the minstrels in their colorful medieval garb. The Bishop had just finished reading the story when in came Monsignor Holstein, who said he'd spotted the men in Hokey's, the town's leading department store, and complained bitterly that they had been singing pagan-inspired drinking songs. The Bishop listened to him but said nothing, and Monsignor Holstein went away. Did it matter to Monsignor Holstein that the minstrels were important men in the community, that they thought they were engaged in a good work, that the *Times* thought so? Monsignor Holstein had just plunged in, as was his habit—a very bad habit. Monsignor Holstein was a rash man, an unsuccessful man, and even when he was right, as he sometimes was, there was something wrong—something wrong about the *way* he was right. However, the Bishop did feel that jolly songs shouldn't be performed under his auspices during Advent, which, as Monsignor Holstein had said, was a

penitential season second only to Lent, and so Father
Gau was asked to see that such songs were dropped
from the minstrels' repertoire, the Bishop citing "Jingle
Bells," and another that, to quote Monsignor Holstein,
went "Ho, ho, ho, the wind doth blow!" When Father
Gau heard these words from the Bishop's lips, he smiled,
and then the Bishop, too, smiled. Until then, he had
been worried that Father Gau might think that the
Vicar-General was running the diocese. Father Gau,
though, had made a joke out of the incident—and, to a
certain extent, out of Monsignor Holstein.

In January, after Monsignor Holstein left town—he was
appointed pastor of St. John Nepomuk's, in New Pilsen
—the Bishop and Father Gau were often seen together
in the evening, in the main dining room of the Hotel
Webb. The food was good and plentiful at the Webb.
The tables weren't placed too close together, there was
light enough to eat by, and there was music. In fact, the
organist, a nice-looking middle-aged woman who didn't
use too much make-up, was a Cathedral parishioner.

These evenings at the Webb, topped off with Bene-
dictine and Dutch Masters, were great occasions for
Father Gau (who called himself a country boy), and
this was a good part of the Bishop's pleasure in them,
although he also did most of the talking. He spoke of his
youth "in and around Fargo," of his years of study at
home and abroad, of his ordination at the hands of a
cardinal in Rome. Back and forth in time he journeyed,
accompanied by Father Gau, who now and then asked a
question. One evening, the Bishop spoke of the curious
role the number two had played in his career: curate in
two places, pastor in two, chaplain to the Catholic
Foresters for two terms, fourth Bishop of Ostergothenburg (and four is the square of two), and consecrated

on his forty-second birthday, on the second day of the second month. "In 1932."

"Gee."

On another evening, the Bishop said, "I couldn't have been more surprised if I'd landed St. Paul or Milwaukee, or more pleased." The Ostergothenburg diocese might well be what it was sometimes called, "the biggest little diocese in the world," for you really couldn't count Europe and South America. There might be dioceses to compare with it in the French part of Canada, but had the faithful in those dioceses been completely exposed to the temptations of a high standard of living? Ostergothenburg, and all the roads around it, blazed with invitations to drink, dine, dance, bowl, borrow money, have the car washed, and so on, but let the diocese stage a rally of some kind at the ballpark and there wouldn't be much doing anywhere else. Oh, of course, if you looked for Ostergothenburg on the map, or judged it by any of the usual rules of thumb—population, bank debits, new construction— you might not think it was much of a place. It had no scheduled air service and no television station and it had lost its franchise in organized baseball. But if you looked at the *diocese*—well, pastors in Minneapolis and St. Paul, who might compare their situations very favorably with those of bishops in barren sees to the north and west, knew they weren't in it with Dullinger. Catholics outnumbered non-Catholics by better than three to one in the diocese. The Bishop had a hundred thousand souls under his care.

"We're well *over* the hundred thousand mark, Your Excellency."

"When I first came here, we were under seventy thousand."

"Gee."

Another man arriving in such a diocese, with no

previous experience as a bishop and only forty-two years old, might have chosen to leave well enough alone. This the Bishop had not done. He had twice voted for F.D.R., had backed the New Deal in all its alphabetical manifestations, and, in general, had tried to do what the government was already doing for the common man, only spiritually. "My words were widely quoted. I was referred to as 'the farmer Bishop.' Some thought it sounded disrespectful. I didn't."

"I don't."

But then had come the war and prosperity. The Bishop went out as before and spoke to gatherings, not so large as before but interested. After the war, to combat the changed times—changed for the worse—the Bishop had reached into the faculty of the seminary for Monsignor (then Father) Holstein.

"We were all sorry to see him go," said Father Gau, who had been a seminarian then.

"A good man, in his way."

Monsignor Holstein had done well with public events of a devotional nature—field Masses, "living rosaries," pilgrimages, and processions. And he had stamped out the practice of embellishing the cars of honeymooners with crude sentiments. But in too many ways he had failed. There had been no change at the Orpheum, and at the normal school some smart alecks who hadn't been organized before—before Monsignor Holstein—now made themselves heard on the slightest provocation. When the second Kinsey report had come out, Monsignor Holstein had played right into their hands, telling the *Times*, "Only an old priest with years of experience in the confessional should write such a book, and he wouldn't." This, though true, had looked silly in print.

The Bishop was glad that the troublesome postwar, or Holstein, period was over. Father Gau had been sta-

tioned at some distance from the front during this period, and might have been interested in a firsthand account of the fighting, but he seemed to understand that
the Bishop didn't care to talk about it.

Father Gau was very understanding. The organist in the
main dining room at the Webb did not forget the
Bishop's one request—for "Trees"—and night after
night played it, sometimes at great length, which was
all right, but when she took to rendering it as a solemn
fanfare to mark his arrivals and departures, the Bishop
wasn't sure he cared for it, but he said nothing. After a
while, the organist abandoned the practice, and Father
Gau, when questioned by the Bishop, admitted that
he'd asked her to do so.

During the day, too, on trips and at the Chancery,
Father Gau saw to it that the Bishop's will was done—
sometimes before the Bishop knew what his will was.
"Just say yes or no, Your Excellency," Father Gau
would say, offering a solution to a problem the Bishop
might not have been aware of, or to one he'd regarded
as tolerable.

One such problem had to do with the regulations for
fasting, which, of all the regulations of the diocese,
were the ones of most concern to the laity. Monsignor
Holstein, trying to make these regulations perfectly
clear and binding wherever possible, had gone too
deeply into the various claims for exemption—youth,
old age, poor health, pregnancy; "But if you *can* fast, so
much the better!"—and had shown an obsessive pre-
occupation with "gravy and meat juices," the abuses of
which were subtle and many. The regulations had been
"clarified" until they were in need of codification and
took a good half-hour in the reading. Father Gau, with

the Bishop's permission, let the wind out of them, and took up the slack with the magic words "If you have any questions, see your pastor."

Father Gau suggested other changes. "You know what, Your Excellency? People don't *know* you." This couldn't be helped, the Bishop felt, but he was interested, and after listening to Father Gau, and seeing that the greater good of the diocese was involved (something he hadn't always been sure about when listening to Monsignor Holstein), the Bishop did promise to be seen more in public. He attended a Bosses' Night banquet given by the local Jaycees, going as Father Gau's guest and giving a talk on "My Boyhood in and Around Fargo," which turned out very well. He kicked off the Red Cross campaign, which hadn't had direct support from the diocese before, and won the approval of non-Catholics, who, economically and ecumenically, were not to be sneezed at, as Father Gau pointed out. The Bishop was even seen at concerts at the two Catholic colleges, which, in recent years, he had visited only when necessary, for commencement exercises, and had departed from as early as he possibly could, as soon as he'd said all he had to say against the sin of intellectual pride. The Bishop really got around. On some nights, returning home, he fell asleep in the car and had to be roused, and it was all he could do to get into his pajamas. But he often retired with a sense of satisfaction he hadn't experienced since his New Deal days.

In his pastoral letters he became more and more humane, urging the faithful to drive carefully, to buy a poppy, to set their clocks ahead for daylight-saving time. Formerly it had been his custom to visit the orphanage once a year, at Christmastime, with six bushels of oranges. He hadn't gone oftener because it always made him feel bad—and mad. Now, at Father Gau's suggestion, he went every month, and found it easier. "They wait for you, Your Excellency," said Father Gau, and he was right.

There were other changes. For some years, the Bishop had had his eye on a certain large family, had noted the new arrivals in the birth column of the *Times*, and had inquired of the family's pastor whether there was any improvement otherwise. (The head of the family was an alcoholic, his wife a chain smoker.) There was no improvement until Father Gau, fighting fire with fire, found the father a job in the brewery. Miraculously, the man's drinking and the woman's smoking fell off to nothing. "There's your model family, Your Excellency," said Father Gau, and the family's pastor agreed. So the Bishop dropped in on the family one Sunday afternoon with a gallon of ice cream, and was photographed with the parents and their fourteen children for the diocesan paper.

And there were other changes. In June, Father Gau, who had been acting rector of the Cathedral, became rector in fact, and a domestic prelate.

"Gee," said Monsignor Gau after the colorful ceremony—at which the choir had performed under the direction of Mr. McKee, whose reappointment had been one of the first official acts of the new rector. "Gee, Your Excellency."

"Just call me 'Bishop.' "

The next day, a scorcher, it was business as usual for the Bishop and Monsignor Gau at the Chancery. In the afternoon they drove out to the cemetery, where the big cross was to be relocated so that it would be visible from the new highway across the river—the Bishop had noticed many out-of-state cars in town during the past week. He had hoped to escape the heat by coming out to the cemetery, but the place just *looked* cool. He walked along the edge of the low bluff, below which ran the river, until he found a spot he liked, and Monsignor Gau marked it with a brick. Then the Bishop gazed around the cemetery with an eye to the future. "I give it ten years."

"If that," said Monsignor Gau.

The Bishop shot a glance at the adjoining property, a small wilderness belonging to the Ostergothenburg Gun Club.

"It's a thought," said Monsignor Gau.

But that evening at the Webb, which was comfortably cool, Monsignor Gau said he doubted if any land at all could be had from the Gun Club, and also if purchasers of cemetery lots would care to be any closer to the activities of the Gun Club. As for buying the Gun Club lock, stock, and barrel (to answer the Bishop's question), even if that could be done, it would be a very unpopular solution. The center of population had shifted north since the war, people following wealth and the river as closely as they could, and now, all along the river, right up to the cemetery and continuing on the other side of the Gun Club, there were these large estate-type houses, while back from the river the prairie was filling up with smaller but still very nice houses. "The Gun Club's holding the line against us, as some people see it, and they'd take us to court if we could get the Gun Club to sell—*if*."

"I had a chance to buy that property long before it was the Gun Club's, and I wish I had," said the Bishop.

"Things go on there at night," said Monsignor Gau.

"What kind of things?"

Monsignor Gau didn't seem to know how to put it. "Shenanigans," he said.

The Bishop just looked at him.

"Cars drive in and park," Monsignor Gau explained. "In fact, there have even been trespassers in the cemetery."

The Bishop sighed. He had heard that such things happened, but not in Ostergothenburg. A high wall? A night watchman? He thought of the cost to the diocese, and sighed again.

"Bishop, don't say yes or no to this right away," said Monsignor Gau. Proceeding slowly, with great caution —as well he might, if the Bishop understood him— Monsignor Gau offered a solution to the problem. For the sake of the town and the diocese, for the sake of the living and the dead, said Monsignor Gau, the Bishop should *move* the cemetery.

"No, no."

"Frankly, I don't see what else we can do, Bishop," said Monsignor Gau.

"Wait a few years," said the Bishop, finally.

"I just thought now, rather than in a few years or ten years from now, might be better, all things considered."

Monsignor Gau, it seemed, hadn't given any thought to the possibility that the Bishop might not be around in ten years. This was comforting, in a way, but it also forced the Bishop to recognize, as he hadn't before, clearly, that it had been his intention to leave the problem of the cemetery to his successor, and, seeing this as a defect in himself, he took another look at Monsignor Gau's solution. No, all the Bishop liked about it was being able to thwart the desires of trespassers. That was all. That, however, appealed to him strongly. "Where?"

"I was thinking of the old airport—high, level ground, good visibility from the road. Hilly, secluded cemeteries were all right in the past."

The Bishop just looked at Monsignor Gau.

"Think of the mower, Bishop."

When the Bishop noticed where they were in the conversation, he didn't want to be there. "The cemetery's consecrated ground," he said.

"Yes," said Monsignor Gau—and did not (which was wise) point out to the Bishop that consecrated ground could be deconsecrated and put to other use in case of necessity. Instead, he spoke of the capacity crowds on Sundays in all four churches in Ostergothenburg, and of the parking problem he had at the Cathedral, which he could do nothing about because of his downtown location. "Oh, I'm not at all *enthusiastic* about moving the cemetery." (The Bishop hadn't realized that they were coming back to that, and sighed.) "Still, if it has to be done, it has to be done."

The Bishop agreed with that statement, in principle, but gave no indication that he did.

"Bishop, don't say yes or no to this right away," said Monsignor Gau, and, having offered his solution to the problem of the cemetery, now offered his solution to his solution: on the consecrated ground, once the mortal remains of the dead had been removed to another location, the Bishop should raise a great church and make *it* his cathedral.

The Bishop said nothing.

"Don't say yes or no right away, Bishop."

No more was said on the subject that evening.

The next morning, at the Chancery, Monsignor Gau entered the Bishop's office saying, "Oh, Bishop, about relocating the cross in the cemetery . . ."

"Better hold off on that. Yes," the Bishop said.

That very day, the Bishop called on Mumm, of Mumm and Muldoon, lawyers for the diocese, and went into the legal aspects of moving the cemetery. It wasn't an easy interview, for Mumm, a man as old as the Bishop, kept coming back to all the paperwork there'd be, as if that were reason enough to abandon the idea. But since the diocese owned the cemetery land, and the graves were only held under lease, subject to removal in case of necessity, there was nothing to stop the Bishop from doing what he had in mind. "Legally," said the old lawyer sadly.

At the Webb that evening, Monsignor Gau, who was working with Muldoon of Mumm and Muldoon, said that Muldoon, whose hobby was real estate, had learned that the old airport could be purchased for only a bit more than the going price for farmland in the area. "Dirt cheap, Bishop. But renting those big earth-moving machines is something else again. We'll need 'em at the old cemetery."

"There'll be a lot of paperwork," the Bishop said, preferring to think of that part of the operation. "And, of course, I'll have to get in touch with Rome."

This he did the next day—entirely on his own, because of a slight difference of opinion with Monsignor Gau over the means to be employed. The Bishop had been going to write to the Apostolic Delegate in Washington, but learned (from Monsignor Gau) that the Apostolic Delegate was in Rome. "Better cable," said Monsignor Gau.

"No, it might give the wrong impression," said the Bishop, who had never, so far as he knew, given Rome that impression.

"To save time," said Monsignor Gau.

"No," said the Bishop, and did not cable.

In his letter, however, he did request that a reply, if favorable, be cabled to him, in view of all that had to be done and the earliness and severity of winter in Minnesota.

After ten days, the reply came. The Bishop let Monsignor Gau read it.

"We're in business, Bishop," said Monsignor Gau. "You *asked* them to cable?"

"To save time," said the Bishop, and their relationship, which had gone off a few degrees, was back to normal.

Things moved quickly then. Letters to the nearest living relatives of those buried in the cemetery and to those, like Mumm, who had contracted for space were drawn up by Muldoon and Monsignor Gau, approved by the Bishop, and dispatched by registered mail. After two weeks, the paperwork was well in hand. During the first week, Muldoon and Monsignor Gau purchased the old airport for the diocese, and the following week it was measured for fencing—galvanized chain link eleven feet high and, as a further discouragement to trespassers, an eighteen-inch overhang of barbed wire. "That should make it as hard to get in as to get out," said the Bishop.

Next, Monsignor Gau and Muldoon, who had been seeing a lot of "the boys at the Gun Club," came to the Bishop and proposed an agreement under which the diocese, soon to have more room than it would need for a new cathedral and perhaps a school later, and the Gun Club, soon to transfer its activities to a location farther up the river, would, for the sake of getting the best price, sell off two contiguous parcels of land as though they were one, as indeed they would appear to be when cleared and leveled, this tract to be restricted to high-class residences only and to be known as Cathedral Heights, with thoroughfares to be known as Cathedral Parkway, Dullinger Road, and Gun Club Memorial Lane. This agreement—over his protests against having a street named after him—was approved by the Bishop. So it went through June, July, and August.

And then, with September and cooler weather, came the hard part for the Bishop, although people who stopped him in the street would never have guessed it. Under his steady gaze, the question that was uppermost in their minds changed from "How could he?" to "How would he?" The Bishop didn't say that he had responsibilities that the ordinary person was neither able to face up to nor equipped to carry out, but he let this be seen. "What has to be done has to be done," he said, "and will be done with all due regard and reverence." And so it was done, in September.

Trucks and earth-movers rolled into the old cemetery, and devout young men from the seminary did the close work by hand. The Bishop was present during most of the first morning to make sure that all went well. Thereafter, he dropped by for a few minutes whenever he could. The Bishop also visited the old airport, now consecrated ground, where clergy in surplices, as well as undertakers and seminarians, were on duty from morning till night. Everything had been thought of (Monsignor Gau, with his clipboard, was everywhere), and the operation proceeded on schedule. After twenty-two days, it was all over, and there was a long editorial in the *Times*.

The Bishop was praised for what he'd done for his town and his diocese, and would do. It didn't stop there. On the street and at the Webb, the Bishop began to see people who had been avoiding him, among them old Mumm, who said, simply, "I got to hand it to you."

And the clergy, too. Men who had stayed away from the Chancery all summer came in again, and some of them, perhaps mindful of the assessments to be levied for the new cathedral, talked up the next parish as they never had before and belittled their own. Some of the Bishop's callers found him not in but at the site of the new cathedral. As long as he had them there, he thought it well to put them in the picture. Pointing to one of the big yellow machines, he'd say, "That one's costing us over two hundred dollars a day. I don't know where it's all coming from, do you, Father?"

On the good days in October and November, the Bishop spent many happy hours at "the job," as it was called. Had bishops in the Middle Ages been so occupied, they might have saved a few years on cathedrals centuries in the building, he thought, for it seemed to him that the men accomplished more when he was around. Some of them he knew from other jobs, and called by name, and others he got to know. One day, he took aside a young workman who was to be married the following morning and spoke to him on the purpose of sex in God's plan, and was so pleased by the response that he gave the young man the rest of the day off and also a cigar, which, since it was a good one, he advised him to save for his honeymoon. Others he spoke to on the purpose of work—a curse, yes, but also a means of sanctification—and cited the splendid example of St. Joseph, a carpenter, the patron of workmen, or workingmen. (The Bishop preferred those words to "worker.") To give additional substance to his remarks, the Bishop spoke of the manual labor he had performed in the years when, home from the seminary for the summer, he'd driven an ice wagon and worked on a threshing crew, and also, though briefly, as a section hand on the Great Northern. "Between Barnesville and Moorhead— until I was overcome by the heat."

By December, the foundation had been poured, the structural steel was in place, and the walls were rising —so slowly, though, that it didn't pay the Bishop to visit the job daily. The men he knew were gone. A few masons drew $4.05 an hour. The Bishop was reluctant to interrupt them. Inside, the air smelled and tasted of oil. Outside, the ground was frozen. By the end of De-

cember, the architects—Frank and Frank, of Minneapolis—and the contractors—Beck Brothers, of Ostergothenburg—were feuding.

The Beck brothers (there were four of them) said
that Frank and Frank, also brothers, were making too
many changes in the plans. If Beck Brothers had known
this was going to happen, they wouldn't have bid on
the job, they said. They hadn't really wanted it. The
plans called for a church such as Beck Brothers had
never built before, or seen. "Too goddam modern," they
said.

None of this reached the Bishop directly, and almost
all of it he discounted, having dealt with contractors for
many years, but one evening at the Webb, early in
February, he mentioned the part that did bother him.

"Frank and Frank are modern, all right, but they're
not *too* modern," Monsignor Gau explained. "Contemporary" was the word for them. They believed in beautiful but simple structures, less expensive, but more
impressive structures, and churches were their specialty.
They'd done churches in such places as Milwaukee,
Dallas, and Fargo, not to mention St. Paul and Minneapolis. "They're tops—and so, locally, are Beck Brothers," said Monsignor Gau.

"Yes, I know," said the Bishop.

"I can tell you what the trouble is, but you can't do
anything about it."

"No?"

"Frank and Frank are from Minneapolis, if you
know what I mean."

The Bishop did. More than once, he'd heard the
contractors refer to the architects as dudes.

The feuding continued into April. In April, the Bishop
was planning to fly to Rome.

By then, the cathedral was beginning to look like something—a chasuble, said the architects; a coffin, said the contractors. It looked like neither, the Bishop thought, and it never would unless you viewed it from above, from an airplane. The Bishop thought that the little model of the cathedral in the contractors' shack could be blamed for much of the trouble—it *did* look like a chasuble or a coffin—and so, on his last visit to the job, before leaving for Rome, he carried it off and locked it in the trunk of the car.

That evening, in the main dining room of the Webb, which he wouldn't see again for perhaps a month, the Bishop got a pleasant surprise, for there, not too close to the organ, having a drink, and soon to break bread together, it seemed, were the two architects and the four contractors. Monsignor Gau was also there, but the Bishop had expected him.

"Well, well," said the Bishop, joining the party. He sat at one end of the table, Monsignor Gau at the other. On the Bishop's right sat an architect, on his left a contractor, and on Monsignor Gau's right and left there was one of each. The seating arrangements had been worked out by Monsignor Gau, the Bishop felt, but how had Frank and Frank and Beck Brothers been brought together?

Presently, this question was answered for the Bishop —and for the Beck brothers, too, to judge by their faces. An architectural journal of excellent repute and wide circulation was planning an article on the new cathedral. If it followed the usual pattern of such articles, said one of the Franks, there would be photographs of the new cathedral and of those intimately associated with the job. "All of us here."

"Why me?" said Monsignor Gau, with a surprised look that didn't fool the Bishop, for obviously Monsignor Gau had heard the good news earlier, had talked it over with Frank and Frank, and on the strength of it had arranged the evening.

"You're rector of the Cathedral—that's why," said the Bishop. "But why me?"

"It's your church," said Monsignor Gau. This was true. In fact, without the Bishop it wouldn't be a cathedral.

The evening now went better. The Beck brothers, who were rather shy men away from their work, opened up as they hadn't before. Frank and Frank said that the food at the Webb surpassed anything Minneapolis could offer and, a little later on, that they wished there were contractors like Beck Brothers in Minneapolis. At that point, the Bishop called for a round of Danish beer, a new thing at the Webb, and they drank a toast to the job.

The Bishop, trying to hold the attention of those at his end of the table, said that they might be interested to know that he had at one time given some thought to building the cathedral out of fieldstone. Yes, plain, ordinary, everyday stones, just as they came from the hand of God and were collected by farmers from their fields. The true and special character of the diocese and its people might be expressed in a cathedral of fieldstones. Monsignor Gau, however, had more or less discouraged the idea, saying that he doubted if fieldstones would look good in a structure of such size, or if fieldstones would hold together as well as, say, bricks. The Bishop had had nothing against bricks, but for a cathedral he preferred stone—good, honest stone. Yes, he was happy with the grey stone that had been chosen. He had wanted a rough finish, yes, until he had learned that this would be too hard to clean, and now he was happy with the smooth. For some reason, perhaps because of his romantic ideas about cathedral-building, he was sorry that the walls wouldn't be solid stone—that the stone slabs, which were being anchored to the steel structure, were only two inches thick. Yes, he'd have reason to be sorry if the walls of the cathedral *were* solid stone—no air space, no insulation. He knew how buildings were constructed now, and wouldn't have it any other way. He wasn't complaining. Yes, he knew that they were doing things with stone that had never been done before, using it as if it were plywood, saving time, labor, and stone, and he was happy. He wasn't complaining. Why should he? He was getting everything he'd ever wanted in a cathedral. It would be ideal for processions—wide aisles, assembly space, space to maneuver in. He was getting landscaped parking lots. He *wasn't* getting as high a structure as he'd wanted at first, but, as Monsignor Gau had pointed out to him, the site would do a lot for the cathedral. From across the river, from the new highway, it wouldn't look anything like Mont-Saint-Michel—another idea the Bishop had had in the very beginning and recognized as crazy even then. In short, he was getting a fine contemporary building with a distinct Romanesque flavor. He was getting real arches. "Oh, I've entirely given up the idea of fieldstones. I wouldn't want 'em now if I could have 'em. But from what I know now, I think it might have been possible."

"Anything's possible, if you're talking about the facing," said the architect on the Bishop's right. "What counts in a building, be it skyscraper or cathedral, is the steel. That's *all* that holds it together."

"Oh, it's *safe*," said the contractor on the Bishop's left. He must have seen that the Bishop could use a little reassurance on that point. "It'll be good for fifty, seventy-five—maybe a hundred—years."

The architect nodded.

* * *

Driving up to the job on his return from Rome (where, except for the Holy Father, nobody had seemed very glad to see him), the Bishop was pleased to note how much had been accomplished in his absence. But then, getting out of the car, coming closer and looking up at the arches, none of which had been completed when he last saw the cathedral, he couldn't believe his eyes. Going inside, he found, of course, that what was true of one arch was true of all—those over the windows, those along the aisles, the one over the baptistery, and, worst of all, the one over the sanctuary. In the middle of every arch there were *two* stones—*where the keystone should have been there was just a crack.*

Had any of the responsible parties been with him then—Monsignor Gau, Frank *or* Frank, or any of the Becks—the Bishop wouldn't have been able to conceal his dismay. He decided to say nothing. In the evening, he consulted the complete set of plans in Monsignor Gau's office—and wished that he hadn't relied so much on just the floor plans, for the plans he was looking at did show how the stone would be set. But they didn't say why.

The next day, at the job, the Bishop approached a workman and said in an offhand manner, "No keystones in the arches."

The workman said that keystones weren't necessary in *these* arches—that steel was all that counted in a building nowadays. From another workman whom he questioned in the same manner the Bishop received much the same reply, and again did not pursue the matter. The following day, an intelligent-looking truck driver, the father of seven, told the Bishop that keystones in the arches would have clashed with the architects' over-all plan. The Bishop nodded, hoping to hear more, but did not. The next day, the Bishop spoke to one of the Becks about cathedral-building in the

Middle Ages, saying in an offhand manner, "I suppose keystones in those arches would've clashed with the architects' over-all plan," and was told that you didn't see keystones much any more. Then for two days the Bishop was out of town, but on his return he tried one of the architects, saying, "You don't see keystones much any more." You did, he was told. You still saw them, and more often than not, if not always, they were ornamental. Out of honesty to their materials and, in the case of the new cathedral, out of a desire to give a light and airy feeling to what was, after all, a very heavy structure, Frank and Frank had rejected keystones. It hadn't been easy to give what was, after all, a very heavy, *horizontal* structure, and a rather low one at that, a *vertical* feeling. That was what the cracks did, and what keystones, apart from being obsolete, would not have done.

That was early in May—a very wet month, as it turned out. At the job, there were signs of erosion and subsidence, and the ground was quickly sodded. Fortunately, the hairline cracks that appeared here and there in the fabric of the structure, and that had to be expected, did not widen.

At the Chancery, there were also signs of erosion and subsidence in the Bishop's relations with Monsignor Gau, but here the hairline cracks (which, perhaps, had been present before) did widen. The work of the diocese went on, of course, but there was much less dining out than there had been. The Bishop didn't enjoy being with Father Rapp, and Muldoon and the others, who seemed to appear regularly at the Webb at Monsignor Gau's invitation, and who, though they gave the Bishop all the attention he could stand, still had a way of excluding him from the conversation. On confirmation trips, more often than not, the Bishop was driven by a curate—the Bishop had given Monsignor Gau a

third one for Christmas. Much as Monsignor Gau enjoyed being with the Bishop, driving him and attending
him, he could seldom manage it that spring. "Chancellor" was no longer a synonym for "chauffeur" in the
Ostergothenburg diocese. Monsignor Gau was chancellor in the proper sense of the word, as well as rector of
the Cathedral, building inspector for the diocese at the
job, and troubleshooter there and everywhere—no man
in the diocese below the rank of bishop had ever been
so honored, trusted, and burdened with responsibility.
Monsignor Gau also ran the newly created Diocesan
Procurement Office.

The D.P.O. stocked, or took orders for, practically
everything a Catholic institution required—school and
office supplies, sporting goods, playground equipment,
sacramental wines. It was saving money for the priests,
nuns, and people of the diocese, but it also made demands on Monsignor Gau's time and energy. He had to
spend long hours with his catalogues and clipboard in
the basement of the high school, and he had to go out of
town on buying trips. There had been one or two too
many of these, it seemed to the Bishop, who hadn't
anticipated any when he authorized the D.P.O., which,
though, was unquestionably a success.

However, when the Bishop had approved the sale of
sweatshirts bearing his coat of arms to seminarians and
clergy, he hadn't anticipated seeing one of these articles, as he did in the middle of June, in front of Hokey's
department store, on the person of a well-developed
young lady. Immediately, he stepped into the lobby of
the Webb, phoned Monsignor Gau, and asked that the
stock of sweatshirts be checked. "No more, when those
are gone," he said, after he'd got the count

"Gee," said Monsignor Gau, but he sought no ex-
planation, and the Bishop offered none.

By June, that was how it was with them. During the

previous winter, at Monsignor Gau's suggestion, the Bishop had become a columnist in the diocesan paper, dealing with events at home and abroad, and more than holding his own, according to Monsignor Gau, Father Rapp, and others. In June, he gave up his column. "No more," he said, again in a way that didn't invite questions. That wasn't all. For over a year, at Monsignor Gau's suggestion, letters of congratulation had been going out to Catholics in the diocese who had done something worthy of the Bishop's attention—an honor defined with great latitude by Monsignor Gau—and then, in June, the Bishop ended the practice. "No more," he said.

The Bishop was sorry that he couldn't think of better ways to assert himself in his relations with Monsignor Gau, and was quite prepared for the consequences. Total obscurity held no fears for him at the moment— not that that would ever be his fate. He just didn't want it thought that he wasn't running the diocese. Or was it already too late—again—for any but the strongest proof? If it was, did he wish to give such proof—again? Monsignor Gau was a very popular man with the people, as well as a very successful one. Monsignor Holstein hadn't been either. And the Bishop was older now.

The Bishop had never felt so out of it as he did late in July, at the dedication of the new cathedral. For many months, Monsignor Gau had been busy with the arrangements—not only bishops from nearby sees were asked to attend but also several archbishops, whose acquaintance, it seemed, Monsignor Gau had made, or almost made, on his buying trips. Two archbishops actually showed up for the dedication, as did an unimportant and indigent Italian cardinal, an added starter, who had more or less invited himself. This, apart from the expense of flying the man in, round trip and first class, from Syracuse (N.Y.), where he had relatives, was unfortunate. He talked a lot of nonsense about rice, having been informed somewhere that this was a major crop in Minnesota, as it was in his part of Italy, and nobody had the nerve to tell him that the only rice in Minnesota grew wild and was harvested by a few Indians.

At the dedication itself, this Prince of the Church played with his handkerchief and closed his eyes during the sermon—which might have been shorter, in view of the oppressive heat, and would have been if the Bishop's train of thought hadn't eluded him twice. Both times, he covered up nicely by reviewing what he'd been saying earlier, once shot ahead on the intended line and once on another just as good. Trying to appeal to everybody present—clergy, nuns, and laity, Catholics and non-Catholics, and even children—he spoke of the splendid progress made by the Church and the country in his own lifetime, reckoning it in terms of Popes and Presidents, a number of whom he'd met or seen and come away from with varying impressions, which he did his best to describe, ranging back and forth between Popes and Presidents, pinpointing the great events and legislation associated with each and, whenever possible, bringing in the diocese. Such an effort would have taxed a much younger man on a cool day. As it was, with the temperature in the nineties, the humidity high, and the robes of his office heavy on him, the Bishop left the pulpit in a weakened condition.

The tour planned for the visiting prelates—first, the seminary and then lunch under the trees unless it rained, then the new cemetery, then the high school, and then back to the cathedral for lemonade and a look at the residential quarters—went on without the Bishop. Monsignor Gau led the tour. The Bishop spent the afternoon in seclusion, trying to recover. Monsignor

Gau phoned. "No, it's just the heat," said the Bishop, and wouldn't have a doctor or an air-conditioner. In the evening, it was Monsignor Gau who presided over the banquet at the Webb.

The Bishop stayed home with the housekeeper's cat. He found it too warm for the cat and the paper, but not before he read that His Eminence (as the *Times* called the wandering cardinal in one place) had landed in "the country of Columbus" with the hope of seeing Niagara Falls and what he could of the frontier, and that he was delighted with Ostergothenburg, which was not unlike Brisbane, with the new cathedral, which was not unlike St. Peter's, with the local clergy and laity, whose good sense and piety were not unlike what he'd been led to expect, and with the Orpheum for exhibiting an Italian film during his visit.

In a black mood, the Bishop wondered whether he shouldn't do away with the D.P.O. Later on, when it must have been about time for cigars at the banquet, and for Monsignor Gau to rise and say once again that though he greatly enjoyed city life, he was a country boy and would be proud and happy to be a rural pastor again, the Bishop wondered whether that shouldn't be arranged. At another point in the evening, thinking he might read awhile, the Bishop went into his office for a book but then forgot why he was there, and stood for some time before a chart on the wall. The chart, which was in the form of a cross, had been made by an artistic nun at Monsignor Holstein's instigation, and showed the spiritual plan of the diocese: bishop at the top of the tree, vicar-general below him, then chancellor, and then to the right, on the right branch, clergy in general, and to the left, on the left branch, nuns, or religious, as they were designated on the chart, and, finally, down the middle, on the trunk of the tree, the laity. The Bishop hadn't really looked at the cross for years, and now saw it as he never had before. What struck him was the favored position of one officer of the diocese. He hadn't noticed it before, or it hadn't meant anything to him before, but the chancellor occupied the very heart of the cross. It seemed to the Bishop that the chart, in that respect, gave a distorted view of the spiritual plan of the diocese. He thought of taking it down. But he didn't. He went back to his bedroom and got into his pajamas.

It rained sometime in the night, and cooled off, and the next day the Bishop was almost himself again.

One night about a month later, in a black mood—it had come to his attention during the day that the senior members of the model family had gone back to their old ways—he was standing before the chart again, and again it seemed to him that it gave a distorted view of the spiritual plan of the diocese. He tried one of the thumbtacks, then another. When he had the chart down, he carried it around for a while, not knowing what to do with it. He didn't care to throw it away. He thought of burning it—respectfully burning it, as one would an old, outdated, or perhaps defective flag. In the end, he rolled it up gently, carried it out to the garage, and put it in the trunk of the car with the little model of the new cathedral.

The next morning, he noticed that the cross was still there, in outline, on the wall, and that same morning he received word that he was getting an auxiliary—something he certainly hadn't asked for and didn't want—and that the man chosen for the job was Monsignor, or Bishop-elect, Gau.

ONE OF THEM

Simpson, a convert, had been well treated in the seminary, given a corner bed in the dormitory, then a corner room with two windows, deferred to in class and out, and invariably he (and two Koreans) had been among those chosen to meet visiting speakers. In fact, Simpson may have been too well treated in the seminary, in view of what was to follow, namely, going out into the world, into parishwork.

The parish, Trinity, was in a still good area of apartment houses and residential hotels. The church (no school) was built of crumbly grey stone in the form of a cross but a cross carrying a load on one shoulder—this

was the rectory attached. The pastor was said to be
something of a hermit, a man of few words.

Simpson took this into consideration the afternoon
he reported for duty, and when the door of the rectory
at last opened to his knocking, and the pastor, whom he
hadn't met before but had seen in processions, a spare,
grey Irish type, just looked at him, Simpson did his best
to display an uncritical nature and a genuine concern
by smiling and frowning at the same time.

"Doorbell out of order, Father?"

The pastor nodded, just perceptibly.

Simpson nodded back—a curate was supposed to
model himself on his pastor—and seeing no need to introduce himself, his suitcases having already done that
better than he could, without words, he entered the dim
hallway. There he placed his suitcases longwise against
the wall so nobody would fall over them, using his head
(the pastor would be glad to see), and then he faced
the office.

But the pastor was making for the stairs.

Simpson swooped down on his suitcases, thinking,
Yes, of course, he was to be shown his quarters first,
after which they'd come down to the office for a little
talk, or maybe the pastor would brief him while showing him around—Simpson saw them up in the choir loft,
down in the boiler room.

The pastor opened a door in the upstairs hallway,
stepped back, and *spoke*. "Room."

Simpson nodded, entered, and placed his suitcases
longwise against the wall, again making a good job of it.
"Nice room," he said, and noticed that he was alone.
Hearing a little noise in the distance like a door closing, he foolishly went and looked out into the empty
hallway. He left his door open in case the pastor was
coming back.

This seemed less and less likely as the afternoon

wore on, and after unpacking, and reading his office, Simpson closed his door and tried his bed. He was there when he heard a knock, just one. Nobody at his door, but footsteps on the stairs, going down. He put on his collar and coat, found the bathroom, and hurried downstairs where he soon found the dining room.

The pastor, seated at the table, greeted him with a nod and introduced him ("Father uh Simpson") to the elderly housekeeper, a small wiry individual ("Uh Miss Burke").

"*Miz*," she said.

The pastor bowed his head in silent grace, as Simpson did then, and while they ate—hashed brown potatoes, scorched green beans, ground meat of some kind—Ms. Burke set the table with things that should have been on it earlier (such as a napkin for Simpson), then appeared at intervals with a loaf of sandwich bread under her arm, put out some (the pastor ate a lot of bread), and disappeared into the kitchen, talking to herself.

"Still sore," said the pastor, silent until then. "Sat where you're sitting. Beeman."

"Father Beeman?" Father Beeman was Simpson's predecessor in the curate's job, an older man, an ex-pastor with, it was said, personality problems.

"Know him, do you?"

"No, but I know what he looks like. I've seen him in processions. Big man."

The pastor nodded. "Threw stuff. Threw his food on the floor."

Simpson nodded.

The pastor shook his head. "At Holy Sepulchre parish now."

"One of my classmates—Potter—*he's* at Holy Sepulchre."

There was no response from the pastor, and no more conversation.

Ms. Burke came in with dessert—sliced canned peaches and cardboard Fig Newtons—and began to remove things from the table.

Simpson thanked her with a nod, almost a bow, when the meal was over, caught up with the pastor in the hallway, and got into step. "Ms. Burke's been with you for some time, Father?"

The pastor nodded, just perceptibly. "Take the eight o'clock Mass, Father. Weekdays."

"Eight o'clock." Simpson repeated it to minimize the chance of error. "Weekdays."

"See about Sundays later."

"Right." It was Simpson's impression that briefing had begun and would continue in the office, which they were approaching, but the pastor kept going, and at the head of the stairs it was Simpson's impression that the man was about to leave him.

"G'night."

"*Father*"—it came out sounding desperate—"I've been wondering about things."

The pastor, on the point of entering the room at the head of the stairs, looked embarrassed. "Uh. Convert, aren't you?"

"No, no. I mean—yes." Simpson had answered the question in order to get back to the assumption underlying it—it was understandable—that he, as a convert, might be shaky in his faith. "No, no, Father, I was just wondering about things—you know, like what time I say Mass." And, quickly, lest that be misunderstood: "Eight o'clock. Weekdays."

"See about Sundays later."

Simpson sort of nodded. "The rest can wait, Father?"

The pastor nodded, just perceptibly, opened the door but not much, and in a crabwise manner that aroused and thwarted Simpson's curiosity, entered the room at the head of the stairs.

*   *   *

The next morning Simpson said the eight o'clock Mass and had breakfast (learned from Ms. Burke that he got Wednesday afternoons off), went upstairs and brushed his teeth, but after that he didn't know what to do. Ms. Burke had made his bed. On the chance that he'd find his orders for the day in the office, he went downstairs and checked it. No, nothing for him. Acting then on information from Ms. Burke, and again using the door he'd discovered, the door between the rectory and the church, he entered the sacristy, and was there when the pastor came in to vest for Mass, there with the idea of bringing himself to the man's attention, and also of being useful, but was told when he attempted to help with the alb, "Not necessary, Father." So he returned to the rectory and, because the pastor could have dropped something off there on his way to Mass, rechecked the office. No, nothing. He then went up to his room and sat down with his breviary, leaving his door open, though, because he was (he thought) on duty. But nobody called at the rectory, or at least nobody knocked, during this period. When he heard footsteps—another reason for leaving his door open—he got up and left his room, again with the idea of bringing himself to the man's attention. He met the pastor at the head of the stairs, was nodded at in passing, nodded back, and went down and checked the office. Nothing.

He wanted to retire to his room and settle down with a good book, but thought it wouldn't look or, perhaps, be right if he did. So he kept coming and going between his room, the office, and the church (with which he was familiarizing himself), and took a side trip down to the boiler room. In this fashion, moving about, looking for the action, he got through the morning.

In the afternoon—lunch, conversationally, wasn't up to dinner the evening before—there were a number of developments:

1. Simpson dealt with several parishioners in the office, with all satisfactorily, he thought, though not to the satisfaction of one, who unfortunately couldn't be helped (marriage case).

2. The pastor emerged from the room at the head of the stairs and left the rectory carrying a brown canvas suitcase such as students once used to mail laundry home.

3. Simpson visited the kitchen for the first time and learned from Ms. Burke, who was having coffee with a middle-aged man to whom Simpson wasn't introduced, that laundry was not sent out, was done right there, and that the pastor used the brown canvas suitcase "to carry his goddam envelopes"—"Oh," said Simpson, and swiftly departed, under the impression that Ms. Burke had been referring to collection envelopes, actually the contents thereof, and that the pastor had gone to the bank.

4. The pastor returned to the rectory with the brown canvas suitcase (but it was apparently no lighter) and entered the room at the head of the stairs.

5. Simpson discovered that the man he came upon (praying?) in the choir loft was the same man he'd seen earlier in the kitchen, and that this man was the janitor —who said he hadn't introduced himself in the kitchen because he and Father Beeman, a real man whose guts Ms. Burke, a holy terrier, hated, had been very close. "I didn't want her to get any ideas about *us*, Father."

Those were the developments that afternoon, some good, some not so good, and one puzzling to Simpson but probably none of his business (the brown canvas suitcase).

That evening, when Simpson came to the table, there was a bad development, a pamphlet—*The Marks of the True Faith*—by his plate.

"Uh. Might interest you."

"Yes, well, *yes*. Thanks."

The silence that set in then—to which Simpson contributed handsomely, rather than try to explain his words of the evening before, his *"Father,* I've been wondering about things," to which words he attributed the pamphlet—lasted until they rose from the table.

"Uh."

"Oh."

Simpson had almost gone off without the pamphlet!

At the head of the stairs, the pastor, silent since alluding to the pamphlet, said, "G'night."

"Father, I've been wondering"—he'd stepped out for tobacco that afternoon, and rather than knock had entered the rectory through the church—"shouldn't I have a key to the front door?"

"Uh. See about it," said the pastor, and entered the room at the head of the stairs in a crabwise manner, the door closing after him.

Simpson waited a few moments there, just in case the door opened and a hand came out with a key, which didn't happen, and so, treading softly, he went down the hallway to his room, his thoughts turning from the key to the pamphlet, which, after brushing his teeth and filling his pipe, he read at one sitting and found excellent.

After a few days, with the pastor keeping to the room at the head of the stairs, Simpson accepted the odd fact that he was on his own at Trinity, stopped looking for the action, and sometimes settled down with a good book—was reading *Enthusiasm: A Chapter in the History of Religion: With Special Reference to the XVII and XVIII Centuries*, by Monsignor Knox (a convert), and shook his head at the hysteria in the Church then, as he did at the hysteria in the Church now, thinking, *Plus ça change* the more it's the same, as he did after trying another position in the hard swivel chair.

The office, where he now had a few of his books and his rubber-tire ashtray, and where he now hung his biretta and stole, he was gradually making his own

The pastor had looked in once to say, "Smoke a pipe, do you?" and twice to say, "Need that light on, do you?" And one afternoon, when Simpson was doing his best to describe the quality of life after death to a curious parishioner, the pastor came all the way in (for a paper clip) and left the door open on his departure—a mistake, Simpson realized then, for him to be alone with a member of the opposite sex (whatever her age) with the door closed, and he didn't let it happen again.

Simpson learned from his mistakes.

Instead of going up to the door of the room at the head of the stairs to announce the arrival of a salesman —had received no response at all the second time he did that—he now dealt with such callers himself in a courteous, businesslike manner, and never bought anything.

He was the same with parishioners if the matter was one on which the Church's position was still clear and negative—some people seemed to think there were now two or more schools of thought about everything. Unlike some newly ordained men, and here perhaps he showed the pastor's influence, he didn't try to say too much. He just tried to do all he could for people, but not *more* than he could (which a visiting speaker at the seminary had called the great temptation to the priest

today), and in pursuing that limited objective he had
his first (and, he hoped, last) confrontation with the
pastor, the man suddenly on the stairs, whispering
down:

"What's this? What's this?"

"Bell."

"*Bell?*"

"Bell. Man fixing it."

"*What?*"

"Bell."

"*Man fixing it?*"

"Is, yes."

"*Called man?*"

"Did, yes."

"*Get estimate?*"

"Sort of."

"*How much?*"

"Not much."

"*How much, Father?*"

"Not much, Father."

There, the pastor retiring to the room at the head of
the stairs, the matter had ended, with Simpson, who,
after all, had called man, paying him (not much) and
keeping the receipt in case he was ever asked for it.

Relations between Simpson and the pastor were the
same as before the confrontation, and this was to the
pastor's credit, but as before there was room for improvement—a sort of gap, like the Grand Canyon, that
had so far defeated all efforts to fill it. Simpson, on his
first Sunday at Trinity, had praised the pastor's sermon,
saying he hadn't heard the like since he didn't know
when (hadn't wanted to say since coming into the
Church), and the man had just nodded, just perceptibly
—not a good sign, Simpson knew now. Taking a chance,
Simpson had asked the pastor where he got his hair cut,

and the man had said, "Anywhere." Taking another chance, Simpson had complimented the pastor on his white teeth, and the man had said, "Don't smoke."

But Simpson was still hoping to fill the gap, still looking around for common ground, and, not finding any, he created some by visiting the zoo (one of the pastor's few outside interests, according to John, the janitor) and came to the table that evening full of it.

"Father, I didn't know they let those big turtles run around loose."

"Tortoises, Father. Harmless."

"Tortoises. But people shouldn't write stuff on their shells."

"Do it here, in the pews."

That had been it for the zoo.

On his next afternoon off, Simpson visited the Museum of Natural History (one of the pastor's few outside interests, according to John) and came to the table that evening full of it.

"Father, how about that big moose by the front door!"

"Elk, Father. *Megaceros Hibernicus.*"

"Elk. Those crazy antlers! Wouldn't want to run into him!"

"Extinct."

That had been it for the Museum of Natural History.

Maybe, if Simpson had had some doubts or difficulties of a spiritual nature, and these had been brought to the pastor's attention, they would have filled the gap, but Simpson didn't have any such doubts or difficulties, and there was little or no audible response from the pastor—a noise like "Umm," or a nod—when Simpson tried to discuss the merits of the pamphlets he continued to find by his plate.

Oh, they were excellent pre-conciliar works, and maybe the pastor would have done as much for any young man fresh from the seminary in times like these . . . but the fact that *Simpson* was receiving such atten- tion, and the fact that *Simpson* was still without a key to the front door—these facts when taken together—did sort of suggest that *Simpson* wasn't trusted, and that troubled him.

Three times he'd raised the matter of a key, and three times he'd been told, "Uh. See about it."

One evening—well into his fourth week at Trinity— he raised the matter again, indirectly, but urgently:

"Father, what if, like tonight, I'm out with my class- mates and I come in late—after nine, I mean—and the church is *locked?*"

" 'M up till 'leven or so. Just knock. Uh. Ring."

So Simpson, a few minutes before eleven that night, rang.

He was determined not to complain. He thought there was too much of that going on these days among the clergy, of all people. He would not, he thought, be happier in another parish, neither in the suburbs nor the slums, for he was not, though fresh from the semi- nary, one of those who expect to change the world by going out into it. For him the disadvantages in his situa- tion were outweighed by the advantages. At Trinity he could feel that he was still in the church of his choice, with divine worship and the cure of souls still being conducted along traditional lines—no guitars, tom-toms, sensitivity sessions, speaking in tongues—and at Trinity he could also feel that he, though newly ordained and a convert, though keyless and considered a suitable case for pamphlets, was the man in charge.

Simpson had visitors one afternoon, Mother and Aunt Edith, and began by showing them the church, which, he could see, disappointed them.

"Yes, it's quite nice," said Mother.

"Why, yes," said Aunt Edith.

"Actually," said Simpson, "it's quite ugly. But it serves its divine purpose, and *that's* the main thing." He felt tough, had sounded the rude Roman note (GIVE ME SOULS!), and had hit a nerve or two, he knew.

"Well, if you say so, dear," said Mother.

"Hell, yes," said Aunt Edith.

Simpson moved toward the sacristy—had taken the visitors into the sanctuary for a close-up view of the main altar—but stopped, hearing a noise from the body of the church, the emptiness of which he'd been regretting for the sake of the visitors (non-Catholics), and saw the middle door of the spare confessional, the door to the priest's compartment, open, and John appear, then disappear into the vestibule.

"Just the janitor," said Simpson.

"Thank *God*," said Aunt Edith.

"Why," said Mother, "he was in there all the time. Did *you* know he was in there, dear?"

"Didn't, no."

"He goes in there to pray, dear?"

"No, he just *goes* in there—to sleep, I think. Maintenance could be better."

"But should he *do* that, dear? In *there*?"

"Oh, what the hell," said Aunt Edith.

"He really shouldn't, no, but we're not rigid in the Church," said Simpson. He took the visitors through the sacristy, his usual route into the rectory, and, since this was their wish, back to the kitchen, where they met Ms. Burke, who could be heard talking to herself again after they left.

"Actually," said Simpson, "she's all right."

He took the visitors into the office ("my headquarters"), where they admired the secondhand *Catholic Encyclopedia* (Unrevised Version) he'd purchased with gift money from the family, and two hard-to-find works by Cardinal Newman (a convert). At Mother's request, he sat for a moment at the desk. "Now I'll know how you look, dear." Aunt Edith tried on his biretta. Then, thinking that later, when they were leaving, would be soon enough to knock at the door of the room at the head of the stairs, he took them to his room, where they inspected his closet, pulled out his dresser drawers, and had the pleasure of seeing and hearing him on the phone with a misinformed but docile parishioner. And then who should walk in (the door was open, though the pastor's open-door policy might not apply in this case) but Ms. Burke with a loaded tray!

Overwhelmed by this womanly display, ashamed of himself for having underestimated Ms. Burke, and thinking it would be a nice gesture anyway, Simpson invited her to sit down, and when Aunt Edith insisted, she did. So Simpson hurried off for another cup, hoping for the best.

When he returned, they didn't seem to notice—they were talking—and since he was the host, he poured, delivered the cream and sugar, the cardboard Fig Newtons, and was shocked to hear Aunt Edith say, sweetly, *"Homemade?"* but she got away with it.

"Pooh," said Ms. Burke. "I just keep 'em in a plastic bag with a clothespin on it."

"And warm before serving?" said Mother.

"I did *these.*"

Simpson tried one of the Fig Newtons, and they *were* slightly better this way. "Umm," he said. Otherwise he contributed nothing to the conversation, just listened along, nodding or shaking his head—detergents did strange things. But after a bit he began to stiffen and was soon rigid. Hearing that "your boy" was easy to cook for, *not* like Father Beeman ("That big *Beer-man!*"), who had thrown his food on the floor, rolled in at all hours, and pounded on walls, and that "your boy" kept his room very clean for a man, and certainly for a priest (Ms. Burke here sniffing in the direction of the room at the head of the stairs), "your boy" regretted that praise for him should be so much at the expense of others. And was afraid that admonishment from him would aggravate what might otherwise pass off as tittle-tattle. To think, he thought, that the pastor had once said to him, speaking of Ms. Burke, who was carrying on with herself in the kitchen at the time: "Uh. Very loyal."

Very loyal to tell the visitors—outsiders, non-Catholics—that the pastor was a pack rat, and wouldn't let her into the room at the head of the stairs to clean? That the pastor was a skinflint, and kept the Christmas ham in the trunk of his car, bringing it out for meals? That the pastor would do anything for a buck, and addressed envelopes for an insurance company in his spare time?

"Tried to get *me* to do it, but I *wouldn't*," said Ms. Burke.

"Why *should* you?" said Aunt Edith. "You've got *enough* to do."

Simpson got up, and moved toward the door.

"You didn't know about the envelopes, dear?"

"Didn't, no."

"*He* thought they were *laundry!*" said Ms. Burke, and smilingly explained how Simpson had made that mistake. "That's how much *he* knew!"

Simpson—who had been suspicious of the brown canvas suitcase from the start and had since seen it too often in transit for it to be going to and from the bank—shut the door, and while this did not have the desired effect, there is some justice in the world and Aunt Edith, over-stimulated, spilled her coffee.

Simpson smilingly scrubbed it into the carpet with his feet, making nothing of it, the good host.

Ms. Burke, concerned about a few drops on Aunt Edith's dress, scurried off to her room for her spot remover.

The visitors went down the hallway to the bathroom for plain cold water.

When Ms. Burke returned from her room, which was adjacent to Simpson's but accessible only by the stairway off the kitchen, she was panting and, not seeing the visitors, gasped: "Gone!"

"No, no," said Simpson.

They regrouped in his room, and after some talk of stains (what it came down to was, no stain should be allowed to *set*, which Simpson planned to use as an argument for frequent confession), the entire company —Ms. Burke saying, "Pooh, I'll clean up in here later"— moved out, and went down the hallway three abreast, one behind, that one thinking, Some other time, as he passed the door of the room at the head of the stairs. But when he opened the front door to let the visitors out, there, about to use his key, was the pastor.

"Uh," he said.

"Uh," said Simpson, and made the introductions.

The visitors were happy to see the pastor, and so was Simpson—to see him there, to think he'd been out, probably at the hospital (one of his few outside interests), while Ms. Burke was assassinating his character with the door open. The pastor was doing as well as could be expected, responding with little nods, and noises like "Umm," to the compliments on his church, rectory, housekeeper, until—suddenly, if you didn't know the man—he made for the stairs.

"Oh, *goodbye!*"

"Why, *yes.*"

The pastor, on the stairs, stopped and turned. " 'M takin' a trip next week."

This was news to Simpson.

"Oh, *where?*" said Aunt Edith.

"Winnipeg."

"Oh, *why?*" said Aunt Edith.

"Catholic Wildlife Conference."

"Oh," said Aunt Edith.

"While you're away," said Mother, "will . . . will *Father*, here, be in charge?"

The pastor, before turning and continuing up the stairs, nodded, just perceptibly.

Simpson was glad to see his authority confirmed, but wished the signal had been a little stronger, for the sake of the visitors, who then left.

Ms. Burke said, "Think they'll come again?"

"It's possible," said Simpson.

"When?"

"Oh, I couldn't say when."

"Soon?"

"Oh, I wouldn't say soon."

"You ask 'em this time?"

"Why, yes, of course."

"Ask 'em again."

"Uh. See about it."

The next evening, while brushing his teeth, Simpson noticed that there had been a blessed event among the towels in the bathroom, twins, two little pink ones.

"Father," said Simpson, coming to dessert, and remembering how he'd phrased the question before ("Father, how long will you be gone?") rephrased it, "will you be gone long?"

"Not long," said the pastor, as before.

"Father," said Simpson when he'd eaten his peaches, "while you're away, if I have to go out at night—hospital or something—and the church is locked, I can knock or ring, I know, but I'd hate to disturb Ms. Burke, if you know what I mean, Father?"

The pastor nodded, as if he did know, but bowed his head in silent grace.

So did Simpson then, and, when they rose from the table, did not forget the pamphlet by his plate. "So I should knock or ring, Father?"

"Ring," said the pastor.

A little later that evening, after the pastor and John departed for the airport, John to drive the car back, Simpson stepped out to do some shopping. When he returned, the front door, which he'd left unlocked, was locked (Ms. Burke), and so, rather than ring, he went through the church. He was carrying a brown paper bag and a six-pack of beer for which he'd spurned a bag because his generation, he understood from the media, was perhaps most admired for its lack of hypocrisy. He reached his room (unseen by Ms. Burke, he believed), opened the potato chips, some of which he shook into a dish after first removing the paper clips and dusting it with his elbow, and then opened the cheese dip, this marked down but still not cheap, probably because it came in an attractive wooden bowl suitable for entertaining. Simpson was entertaining two of his classmates, Potter and Schmidt, that evening. He had brought up his rubber-tire ashtray earlier.

When Schmidt arrived with a surprise guest, a Father Philippe, an older man who belonged to a small order recently expelled from one of the developing countries, Simpson hoped to hear something of the Foreign Missions (little discussed these days), but Father Philippe's English was poor, and Potter made the usual

remarks about Rice Christians and Spiritual Colonial-
ism, and dominated the conversation.

So Simpson heard more about the developments
taking place in the Church, notably in Holland, which
he'd heard so much about from Potter and other activ-
ists in the seminary, and then more about the developments taking place at Holy Sepulchre, Potter's parish,
"exciting" being Potter's word for these developments,
"depressing" being Simpson's.

"Look, Simp," Potter said, "we have to do all we can
to extend our outreach—to use a term widely used in
the Protestant churches." Women were now allowed to
take up the collection at Holy Sepulchre, and strobe
lights had been ordered for the sanctuary ("We have to
think of the kids"), and Potter and his pastor, who was
under Potter's influence, were hoping to get Holy
Sepulchre changed to Holy Resting Place as less off-
putting to the churchless. Potter and his pastor were
also hoping that it would soon be possible for people to
fulfill their obligation to attend Sunday Mass not only,
as now, on Saturday but also on Friday or *Thursday*, a
better day, since so many people took off for the lake, or
started drinking, right after work on Friday. Potter and
his pastor were making an effort to keep the confessional doors—the doors to the priest's compartment—
open when the confessionals were not in use, to show
the people, to bring home to them the idea, that God
("Jahweh" to Potter) was not within but on the altar.

"Wow," said Schmidt, who was under Potter's influence.

"No, no," said Simpson. He assured Father Philippe
that keeping the confessional doors open was not a local
custom, nor was it a growing one, as Potter would have
allowed a stranger to believe (all in the day's work for
the enthusiast), and for this Simpson was frowned on
by his classmates.

Potter produced a copy of the Holy Sepulchre parish bulletin, the entire contents being just one word spread over four pages, a letter to a page, LOVE.

"Wow," said Schmidt.

"To think we've come to this," said Simpson, shaking his head, but, thinking the "we" might be resented by his classmates, cradle Catholics, he said to Father Philippe, "I'm a convert, Father."

"Simp, you should do something about your triumphalism," said Schmidt.

"Simp and Lefty," said Potter, and likened Simpson to Father Beeman: *he* had called the LOVE issue a waste of recycled paper but a step in the right direction (*he* wanted no bulletin at all), and *he* was almost certainly the one who kept shutting the confessional doors. "A real cross, that guy, and I'm afraid he knows your pastor's away."

"So?" said Simpson.

"He said he might drop by tonight."

"Oh?" said Simpson—he'd been worried enough before, about the beer running out.

"He might not come," said Schmidt, but he was a Teilhardian optimist.

Father Beeman came, appeared at Simpson's door with John, who was carrying a bag of ice cubes, and was himself carrying a brown paper bag that obviously concealed a bottle. "Surprise," he said.

"No, you're expected, Father. In fact, I was just going out for beer."

"Beer?" said Father Beeman. "Missionary?" he said, when introduced to Father Philippe. "Why aren't you in Holland?" He held up a hand for silence, cupped an ear to hear what Potter, who was ignoring him, was saying to Schmidt, commented "I got your old outreach," and handed Simpson the bottle.

Simpson had to go down to the kitchen for glasses

(he had invited John to stay), and while down there heard the light in the back stairway snap on from above (Ms. Burke), but he did not have to go out for beer. No, as Simpson saw it, those so inclined could simply switch to the bottle when the beer was gone.

And that was what happened, the evening then turning into more of a party, without, however, coalescing —there were still two conversations.

Simpson was in the one with Father Philippe, John, and Father Beeman, who controlled it, not by doing all the talking as Potter had done earlier, but by changing the subject frequently, giving others a chance to be heard briefly. Father Beeman also kept a tap on the other conversation, and occasionally issued a *monitum* ("It's always been a hotbed of heresy, Holland") or posed a question ("What's so relevant about saying Mass in a barn in Belgium?"). Father Beeman also served as bartender to the entire room, a good thing, since Simpson wouldn't have known how much to put in. Father Beeman and his bottle added a lot to the evening, and made it go as it hadn't before. He appeared to be interested in Simpson.

Yes, for when Potter moved down to the floor, into the lotus position, and, at his request, Simpson, who had been sitting on the bed, moved into the vacant chair, which put him with Schmidt in easy range of Potter's voice, he found that he was still regarded as one of Father Beeman's claque (by Father Beeman), and had to attend to two monologues that seemed to be on a collision course.

Father Beeman said, "I don't blame the young clergy for what's happened to the Church, even the screwballs and phonies."

Potter said, "Just because the Protestants do it, is *that* what's wrong with hymn-singing? Next to a married clergy, I'd say *that's* what we need most."

Father Beeman said, "I blame the older men, pastors like the one where I am now—no hair on his head, just sideburns, and those industrial glasses that make *any* man look like an insect."

Potter, wearing such glasses, said, with some difficulty, gulping, "You're the one . . . Lefty . . . shuts those doors." And stood up, with some difficulty.

Father Beeman, looking belligerent and (Simpson thought) guilty, said, "*What* doors?" And stood up.

"Uh," said Simpson, and was wondering what he, as host, should do, and was also recalling what a visiting speaker at the seminary had said, that the greater incidence of fist fights between members of the clergy since Vatican II was yet another sign of the times, and perhaps of the end, when . . .

Father Philippe stood up, and, going over to the wall and standing with his back to everybody, began to disrobe . . . collar, coat, dickey . . . then turned, and displaying his T-shirt, the blue and gold seal of a university thereon, cried, "*Voilà! Souvenir de Notre-Dame!*"

Ms. Burke could be heard pounding on the wall!

"She *still* do that?" roared Father Beeman, and went to the wall and pounded back.

"Uh," said Simpson.

Ms. Burke could be heard again.

"*Listen* to her!" whispered Father Beeman, but did not pound back. "Don't let her push you around, Simpson. See that man there?" (Yes, Simpson saw John.) "She *runs* that man. *And* the pastor. But she didn't run *me.* So don't let her run *you*, Simpson. Be like me."

Simpson sort of nodded.

When Potter, who had left the room when the pounding began, returned, he looked pale and said, "I think it was that cheese dip, Simp."

"Nothing wrong with that cheese dip," said Father Beeman.

Simpson saw Potter, Schmidt, and Father Philippe down to the front door, and returned to his room, wondering why Father Beeman and John were staying, and, again, why they had come.

The answers to those questions were not immediately forthcoming, and Simpson soon forgot those questions, for he heard some very interesting things from Father Beeman and (until he fell asleep) John. *That* the insurance company the pastor addressed envelopes for was Catholic owned and oriented, which Simpson was glad to hear, though he still felt uneasy about such employment for a parish priest and could only accept, in principle, Father Beeman's argument that the pastor was a priest-worker. *That* John had another job, as a night watchman in a warehouse ("Security," he said), which in a rash moment he'd boasted of to Ms. Burke, and now lived in fear that she'd inform the pastor, Father Beeman doubting this ("Suits her better this way"). *That* Ms. Burke, who received a prewar salary like John, never cashed her checks, and this, quite apart from its salutary effect on the pastor, Simpson considered a meritorious practice, even after Father Beeman discounted it ("Hell, she owns a four-hundred-acre farm"). *That* Father Beeman believed the pastor's fine sermons to be the product of reading rather than living, to be thought out, perhaps even written out, before delivery, which struck Simpson as a very Roman view of preaching. *That* the pastor had been active in the so-called streetcar apostolate, this terminated when buses replaced streetcars, buses not having any windowsills to speak of, or the kind of seats on which literature could safely be left—which started Simpson thinking. . . .

"Father," he said, taking a chance, "when you were

here, did the pastor ever—how shall I put it?—put pamphlets by your plate?"

"At first."

Good news for Simpson!

Father Beeman frowned at Simpson (who had been smiling at him). "But I never felt he was trying to straighten me out—and I came here under a cloud."

"Oh?" But Simpson was only interested in hearing about the pamphlets. " 'At first,' you say?"

"Not at the end. I left here under a cloud."

"Oh?"

"Trouble was, he kept his door open at night—he still do that?"

"Oh, no."

"Well, he did when I was here. I used to come up the stairs in the dark—so as not to disturb him—carrying my shoes. Never made it. 'Is that you, Father?' That's what he'd say. Night after night. One night, I'm sorry to say, I let him have it—threw a shoe."

"*Oh?*" Simpson was shocked, but tried not to show it.

"It didn't hit him."

"Oh."

Father Beeman rattled his glass. "*So,*" he said, "I wouldn't worry about the pamphlets if I were you. I can see how you might. But don't. You've got what it takes, Simpson. Or what it did. *You* would've made it through the seminary in the old days—*un*like your classmates who were here tonight and wouldn't have lasted a week. Hell, I wouldn't be afraid to introduce *you* to *my* classmates."

This was high praise to one who'd wished for years at the seminary, and for weeks at his first parish, not to be an object of special concern, neither of charity nor of suspicion, to his dear brothers in Christ, but simply to be one of them, and that praise, coming as it did from one who, whatever his faults, and we all have our faults, was certainly one of them, made Simpson blush.

"I've had *very* good reports on you, Simpson."

Simpson said that several parishioners had mentioned Father Beeman to him (*"How?"*), oh, favorably (*"Who?"*), and supplied a couple of names, after which while John slept on, they sat on, finishing the bottle and discussing the Church, as many must have been doing at that hour in rectories.

"Well, Simpson. Say, what's your first name anyway? Heard those clowns calling you Simp. Didn't care for it."

"Fitch," said Simpson.

Father Beeman brought his glass, empty except for ice, down from his mouth with a clunk.

"It's a family name," said Simpson.

"Well, Simpson, I was sorry for you tonight—her acting up like that in front of everybody. Still, it happened to me when I was here, if that's any consolation to you."

Simpson sort of nodded.

"Don't let her run you. That's the main thing. Don't let her get anything on you. That's the main thing. But *if* she does don't let her run you."

Simpson sort of shook his head.

"Well, Simpson." Father Beeman glanced at his watch, became interested in the back of his hand, tasted it, dried it on his sleeve, and got up, saying, "Nothing wrong with that cheese dip." He woke John (who had to go to his other job and for whom he'd been watching the time), and then he handed Simpson a key, saying, "Carried it away."

Good news for Simpson!

The evening, though dull at first with Potter doing

all the talking, and bad at one point with Ms. Burke acting up like that, had certainly ended well, Simpson was thinking, as they went down the hallway, when Father Beeman stopped and said:

"The thing is, Simpson, I never got my shoe back."

Hearing this, and seeing where they'd stopped in the hallway, Simpson was shocked, but tried not to show it, and quickly made his position clear. "Afraid you'll have to see the pastor, Father."

Father Beeman said, "Should've said something at the time—the next day, or the day after. But you know how these things are, Simpson—the longer they go on, the worse they get. We weren't talking at all—not that that was much of a change. You know how he is. Was going to say something the day I left, but thought, No, why embarrass him, why embarrass us both?"

"Afraid you'll have to see the pastor, Father."

Father Beeman said, "Look, Simpson, how'd you like to have one shoe, and know where its mate is, and not be able to lay your hands on it?"

"Afraid you'll have to see the pastor, Father."

"Look, Simpson. It's *my* shoe. Come on, John. Help me hunt."

John did.

Simpson walked up and down the hallway, and having had his first look into the room at the head of the stairs—an indoor dump—and hearing Father Beeman tell John the shoe wasn't where it should be (*"Going by the flight pattern"*), he began to hope that it wouldn't be found, which would be best for all concerned.

"How about that? He must've picked it up!"

Father Beeman came forth with the shoe, looking pleased with himself, and under the impression that Simpson wished to shake his hand

Simpson gave him back the key.

"Look, Simpson, this is *your* key."

Simpson casually put his hands behind him and held them there.

"Wouldn't want to say where you got it?"

"In the circumstances, no."

"O.K., Simpson." And Father Beeman gave the key to John.

"Put the shoe back, Father," Simpson said, "I'm in charge here now."

"Look, Simpson, *this* is *my* shoe. Good shoe, too. Bostonian. Hell, it'll never be missed in *there*. Even if he misses it, which he won't, he'll just think it's lost. You won't have to say I was here."

Simpson, remembering the pounding, shook his head.

The pastor and Simpson ate their hashed brown potatoes, scorched green beans, and ground meat of some kind, and Ms. Burke set the table with things that should have been on it earlier, then appeared at intervals with a loaf of sandwich bread under her arm, put out some (the pastor and Simpson ate a lot of bread), and disappeared into the kitchen, talking to herself—a typical meal, nothing unusual about it, except the collection of airline condiments and comestibles at the pastor's place. The pastor had come to the table straight from the airport, and Simpson, though he'd come to the table after the pastor that evening, doubted that there had been time for Ms. Burke to report what had happened at the rectory while the pastor was away, not long, not quite forty-eight hours.

"What was your trip like, Father?"

"Turbulence."

"Oh?" And Simpson thought of the turbulence at the rectory during the pastor's brief absence. The worst thing, in a way, was that one of Simpson's guests, prob-

ably Potter, had used the little pink towels in the bathroom. These Simpson, before retiring that night, had
noticed in the bathtub, had smoothed out, folded, and
hung up where they belonged, but in the morning, wak-
ing with what he could only assume was a hangover,
he had found them gone. Alluding to them at breakfast
—"Uh. One of my guests . . ."—he had received no
response from Ms. Burke; and then he had, a bitter one.
"I know *who* was here, and I know *why*." "I," Simpson
had replied, and had been going to say *I tried*, but the
thought of his failure to protect the pastor's interest had
silenced him. Ms. Burke hadn't spoken to Simpson since
then, and he hadn't spoken to her. His idea was not to
let her intimidate him, not to let her run him. What he
had lost with Ms. Burke in the way of respect, he had
gained in camaraderie with John, who—overly solici-
tous about Simpson's "head," comparing it with his own,
and with some heads he'd had in the past (in some of
which Father Beeman had figured), and spending more
time in the combination chair-coatrack-umbrella stand
just outside the office, and less time in the spare confessional—had become a nuisance by the end of that day,
a long day. Simpson had gone to bed early, and was
planning to do so again. There could be something in
what John said, that the second day after could be
worse than the first. "Air turbulence, Father?"

The pastor nodded. He was eating his dessert.

So Simpson picked up his fork.

Ms. Burke came into the dining room. "What!" she
cried, breaking her great silence where Simpson was
concerned. "Eatin' peaches with a fork?"

"No spoon," said Simpson, breaking his great silence
where Ms. Burke was concerned.

"No *spoon*?"

"No spoon."

"Look on the floor!"

"Looked." To be sure of his ground, Simpson looked again.

Ms. Burke, who had been looking on the floor, gave up and went to the sideboard, again rebuking Simpson. "Eatin' peaches with a fork! You see that, Father?"

"Use spoon," said the pastor.

"Don't have one," said Simpson.

Ms. Burke popped one down on the table, sort of sleight of hand. *"There!"*

"Thanks," said Simpson.

"Pooh!" said Ms. Burke.

"Uh," said the pastor.

Simpson finished dessert, said silent grace, and left the table with the pastor. They drove down the hallway at their usual clip, and were making for the stairs, Simpson thought, when the man suddenly turned out of his lane, saying "Uh." Simpson followed him into the office and, a moment later, thought *this* was how he'd imagined it on his first day at Trinity, the pastor at the desk, himself in the parishioner's chair—and wished he'd emptied his rubber-tire ashtray.

"Talk," the pastor said, still looking at the ashtray.

"*I*," said Simpson.

"Women," the pastor said—evidently had meant that he would, and not that Simpson should, talk—"still great force for good in the world, Father. Be worse place, much worse, without 'em. Our Blessed Mother was one." (Simpson nodded, though the pastor wasn't looking at him.) "Have to watch ourselves, Father. As men. More. As priests. Get careless. Get coarse. Live like bears. Use spoon, Father. Peaches. No spoon, ask for one. Father"— the pastor was looking at Simpson—"don't use guest towels."

"*I*," said Simpson, and was going to say *didn't*, but didn't.

"In future," the pastor said, mildly.

"*I*," said Simpson. "Won't."

The pastor nodded. He rose from the desk.

And Simpson rose swiftly and gladly and guiltily from the parishioner's chair.

The pastor handed Simpson a key. "It turned up."

"Oh, thanks, Father."

"Visit hospital, Father?"

"Did, yes. Twice. Everybody's fine."

They left the office then, and made for the stairs, the pastor's step quickening—Simpson's, too—at the sound of Ms. Burke's voice in the distance (rebuking John), but Simpson was grateful to Ms. Burke for not telling the pastor more than she had, and wondered how he could reward her.

While brushing his teeth, Simpson noticed that the little pink towels were back.

MOONSHOT

A play in three acts

MOON BUILDINGS—*Jack Green, a North American Aviation scientist, said moon explorers might be able to
construct buildings with pumice dust, a hard, powdery
substance that may exist around volcanic craters on the
moon. In a report for a meeting in Washington, D.C., of
the American Astronautical Society, Green said it might
be possible to shape the dust into blocks. These could be
held together by a "waterless cement," obtained from sulphur, which is also believed to exist on the moon.*—Minneapolis Morning Tribune, January 17, 1962.

* * *

Cast

TOM BROWN, a young scientist.

HUB HICKMAN, his friend, a young astronaut.

SENATOR HODGKINS, chairman, Senate Committee on Oceans, Rivers, Lakes, Harbors, and Space.

SENATOR WOODROW, his friend, a member of the Committee.

SENATOR MELLER, a member of the Committee, of another party.

NANCY, Senator Hodgkin's pretty daughter and secretary.

SOPHIE, Senator Woodrow's pretty daughter and secretary.

SERGEANT AT ARMS, PRESS, TELEVISION, and RADIO PEOPLE, LOBBYISTS, SPIES, STUDENTS OF GOVERNMENT, CHAPERONES and SCHOOLCHILDREN, and OTHERS.

Act One

Time: Now

Place: A crowded hearing room, Washington, D.C.

HODGKINS (*continuing*): You a friend of Jack Green?

TOM: No, sir.

HODGKINS: But you know him, don't you?

TOM: No, sir. I don't.

HODGKINS: Don't tell me you haven't heard of him.

TOM: I won't say I haven't heard of him, sir.

HODGKINS: I thought not.

MELLER (*coming to*): Not so fast, Senator. Who's Jack Green?

WOODROW: A North American Aviation scientist.

HODGKINS: And these are *his* ideas that this fella's putting forward. What's your name again?

TOM: Brown, sir. Tom.

MELLER: You're a young scientist?

TOM: Yes, I am, sir.

MELLER: Employed by?

TOM: Self-employed, sir.

MELLER: And your friend also?

TOM: Yes, sir. He's a young astronaut.

HUB (*rising*): Glad to make your acquaintance, sir.

MELLER: Glad to make *your* acquaintance, young man. I'm always glad to meet a young astronaut. Now these ideas, Tom—are they yours or somebody else's?

TOM: I wouldn't claim them as my own, sir. I doubt that anybody would. It's been known for a long time in this country—and in others, unfortunately—that moon explorers might be able to construct buildings with pumice dust.

HODGKINS (*rapping table*): Quiet! You people will please remember that you're here as guests of the Committee.

MELLER: What is this pumice dust, anyway?

TOM: It's a hard, powdery substance that may exist around volcanic craters on the moon.

MELLER: I'm not sure I understand.

TOM: It's believed that it might be possible to shape the dust—or p.d., as it's called—into blocks.

MELLER: Blocks?

TOM: Blocks, sir. These could be held together by a "waterless cement"—not to put too fine a point on it—obtained from sulphur.

MELLER: Sulphur?

TOM: Yes, sir. Sulphur also is believed to exist on the moon.

HODGKINS: I'm surprised you didn't know this, Senator.

WOODROW: I'm not.

MELLER: This isn't my only committee, gentlemen.

HODGKINS: This isn't *my* only committee.

WOODROW: Or mine.

HODGKINS: Nancy, see that the Senator gets copies of a report for a meeting in Washington, D.C., of the American Astronautical Society.

NANCY: Oh, all right.

WOODROW: Sophie, will *you* see that the Senator gets copies?

SOPHIE: Why do I have to do everything? Oh, all right.

MELLER: Thank you.

HODGKINS (*looking toward door*): Who're all those people? Never mind. I thought they were coming in here. Well, Brown, we'd like to be of service to you, of course, but, as you know, this Administration is dedicated to economy as well as security, and we need every penny we have for projects under way—for *regular* agencies of the government. If there was anything really new in your approach, or if you'd actually made the trip to the moon and back, it might be different.

Act Two

Time: Later

Place: The Moon

HUB: Any luck, Tom?

TOM: It's easy enough to get the dust shaped into a block, but as soon as you turn your back something happens to it.

HUB: We're using too thin a mixture, you think?

TOM: Too thin, or too rich, or conditions aren't right—or something! It won't hold. How you comin'?

HUB: Well, this one worked up better than the last. The question is will it hold any better. Nope.

TOM: One more try, to use up what we've got on hand here, and then I'm turning in. We've had a long day, Hub.

HUB: You can say that again.

TOM: Round up some more p.d. and sulphur, so we can get an early start tomorrow. Go ahead, Hub. I'll clean up here.

HUB: Thanks, Tom. You're a brick.

TOM: That last batch of sulphur seemed to have more to it.

HUB: There's plenty more where that came from. (*Goes off.*)

TOM: Don't go too far away, Hub. It's getting dark.

Act Three

Time: Later

Place: A crowded hearing room, Washington, D.C.

HODGKINS: Brown? Who's he? How'd he get scheduled?

WOODROW: I'm sure I don't know.

MELLER: Don't look at me.

HODGKINS: Brown, if you're Brown, who scheduled you?

TOM: I'd rather not say at this time, sir. When you hear all we have to say, sir, I think you'll understand.

HODGKINS: *We? Who's we?*

TOM: My friend and I.

WOODROW: Is your friend present?

HUB: Yes, sir. Hickman, sir. Hub.

HODGKINS: Who scheduled *you*?

HUB: We've just returned from the moon, sir.

HODGKINS (*rapping the table*): Quiet! You people will please remember that you're here as guests of the Committee.

MELLER: *Tom* Brown?

TOM: Yes, sir.

MELLER: Is it true, Tom, that you've just returned from the moon?

TOM: Yes, sir. Actually, we've been back about a week.

HODGKINS (*rapping the table*): Now see here—*quiet!*

HUB: We wanted your committee to be the first to know, sir.

CYNICAL REPORTER: They came to the right place.

TOM: We would've come sooner, sir, but couldn't get past your administrative assistants.

HUB: And legislative assistants, sir.

HODGKINS: I'm always available.

WOODROW: Me, too.

MELLER: Just the two of you made the trip, Tom?

TOM: Yes, sir. There wasn't room for more, what with all the gear. It's just a little two-seater, Hub's heap. Supercharged, of course.

WOODROW: What kind of cock-and-bull story is this?

MELLER: My witness, Senator. And how was it on the moon, Tom?

TOM: About as expected, sir. Dusty. Airless, and therefore soundless, but we used sign language, and later lip reading. Hot during most of the day and cold at night. No rain to speak of while we were there, no moonquakes, and only an occasional meteor hit— none very close to us, fortunately.

HUB: Don't you believe it, Senator. Tom had one near-miss.

TOM: I'd say the hardest thing about it was the duration

of the days and nights—each day, each night lasting two weeks. This made for a long workday, to say nothing of the time spent in the—pardon the expression—sack. But our bodies soon got used to it. Our thoughts were often of home.

HUB: You can say that again.

TOM: And of course it took a while to get used to the buoyancy. I weighed thirty-two and a half pounds, but had the full use of my strength, and a corresponding bulge on matter, which made our work a lot easier than it would have been otherwise.

MELLER: What was your work, Tom?

TOM: Constructing buildings, sir, with pumice dust. We had a devil of a time at first. Couldn't get the p.d., as it's called, to mix properly with the stickum—this obtained from sulphur, which is abundant on the moon, though in varying strengths, so that you have to know what you're doing. We ran quality tests constantly. Once we got the hang of it, we were all right.

MELLER: Did you construct a building?

TOM: Two, sir. Oh, nothing like this one, but good and solid and not too small at that.

HUB: About the size of a bank.

TOM: But for the buoyancy factor, these buildings might have taken the two of us years to complete.

HODGKINS: Who scheduled you two birds?

WOODROW: I've had enough of this.

MELLER: Not so fast, gentlemen. Any signs of other life, Tom?

TOM: If you don't mind, sir, I'd like to reply to the other Senator. We took the precaution to document our trip, fully expecting to be treated as we have been by some here today, though (to Meller) not by you, sir. Photographs of the buildings, samples of the soil, if you can call it that, p.d., sulphur, and so on—actually very little else.

HODGKINS (*rapping*): Quiet!

TOM: Now, sir, to your question. Yes, as you *might* expect if you keep up with the developments in the interstellar field, there were signs of other life on the moon.

HODGKINS (*rapping*): Here! Here! Order! Order!

MELLER: Pray continue, Tom.

TOM: With your kind permission, sir. Signs of other life, yes, and more than signs!

HODGKINS (*rapping*): Sergeant, do your duty. Order! Order! Order!

MELLER: You mean *they* are there?

TOM: Yes, sir.

MELLER: You saw them, Tom?

TOM: Yes, sir, and so did Hub.

HUB: Yes, sir.

TOM: In great numbers, sir. In very great numbers. They did not see us, but we saw them.

MELLER: What were they doing, Tom?

TOM: Why, constructing buildings with pumice dust, sir.

MELLER: How many buildings would you say they have?

TOM: Well, sir, when we left they had the beginnings of only one. Doubtless they ran into the same trouble we did at first, but, like us, they overcame that trouble. How many buildings they have now—with *their* program—I could not say. If I could, sir, I would not care to say in such a public place as this.

CYNICAL REPORTER: Well, I'll be darned!

HODGKINS (*seeing a man trying to slink out*): Stop that man!

SERGEANT AT ARMS: Oh, no, you don't!

MAN: Чёрт возьми! ["Devil take it!"]

HODGKINS (*seeing another man trying to slink out*): Stop *that* man!

SERGEANT AT ARMS: Oh, no, you don't!

MAN: 怎么办? ["What's to be done?"]

HODGKINS: Lock the doors! Lock the doors!

MELLER (*presently*): Well, gentlemen? What do you say now?

HODGKINS: My hat's off to you, young man.

TOM: Thank you, sir.

HODGKINS: And to you, too, young man.

HUB: Thank you, sir.

WOODROW: Same here to both of you.

MELLER: You see, Tom and Hub, they really aren't so bad. Whatever our party differences, we never fail to close ranks when threatened from without. What we have to do now is get that little machine of yours into production.

HODGKINS: And put a million men on the moon constructing buildings with pumice dust.

WOODROW: Two million.

MELLER: Three.

HODGKINS: I still don't know who scheduled you young men.

TOM: You haven't heard *all* we have to say, sir.

HUB: What Tom means, sir, is that he'd like your daughter's hand in marriage.

TOM (*to Senator Woodrow*): And what Hub means, sir, is that he'd like *your* daughter's hand in marriage.

HODGKINS: You mean it was Nancy who scheduled you, Tom?

TOM: Yes, sir.

WOODROW: And it was Sophie who scheduled you, Hub?

HUB: Yes, sir.

HODGKINS: Well, in that case, I don't see why not.

WOODROW: I'll go along with that.

CYNICAL REPORTER: Let me out of here!

PRIESTLY FELLOWSHIP

The time to plant grass seed is in the winter, the man in the next parish had told Joe: just mix it in with the snow and let nature do the rest. So Joe had done that—had believed a priest who rode a scooter and put ice cubes in his beer—and, toward the end of April, had ordered sod. When he discovered that leftover sod couldn't be returned for credit, he'd had it laid down alongside the church, over the flower beds—things like petunias—and now, on a warm Sunday, he could walk in what shade there was during the last Mass, read his breviary, and keep an eye on the parking lot. *The story is told . . ."*

And when the church windows were open, as they were now, he could catch the sermon. He had heard his curate, Bill, earlier, and now he was hearing the old monk who helped out on weekends, Father Otto. *"In like manner, my good people, one part of the camel's corpus was followed by another (indeed, it could not be otherwise) until, at last, the rough beast was inside the tent, and the merchant, poor man, with all his good intentions, was out in the raging desert storm, or simoom. How. Like. Sin. That. Is."*

While Father Otto took it from there, Joe moved out of range, out into the sun. Crossing the parking lot, he paused before a little pile of cigarette butts in the gravel, thought of inspecting the ashtrays of the nearest cars, thought again, and moved on toward his new rectory, thinking, As this church is the house of God, my good people, so this parking lot is—forget it. "You're good people," he called to a young couple. "Good and late." No response. People who'd once been able to take and even enjoy a little friendly needling from their pastor, like the customers in a night club where an insulting waiter is part of the show, were restless and crabby nowadays. They wanted their "rights," expected a priest to act like a minister, to say things like "So nice to see you" and "So glad you could make it," and still they emptied their ashtrays in his parking lot. Entering the rectory by the back door, he washed his hands at the kitchen sink, then slipped into his illustrated apron, wearing it inside out over his cassock so the funny stuff was hidden, and set about making Father Otto's breakfast.

When Bill, on his way over to church to help Father Otto with Communion, passed through the kitchen, Joe looked up from the breadboard, from sawing an orange, and said, "This isn't for me"—just as he had a few weeks back, anxious then to explain his continuing presence in the kitchen to Bill. (It had been Bill's first Sunday at the rectory.) "This isn't for me" had since become something of a family joke, the thing to say when making another nightcap, when not declining dessert, which showed what a good guy Joe was, for he had a slight eating problem, unfortunately, and also a slight drinking problem.

As Bill went out the back door, Joe intoned, *"The story is told . . ."* Father Otto's sermons had become something of a family joke, too. There should be others in time.

Fifteen minutes later, Father Otto passed through the kitchen, and breakfast—or brunch, as he sometimes called it with a chuckle—was served in the dining room. Joe and Bill ate in the kitchen on Sunday, the housekeeper's day off, but Joe felt that Father Otto deserved better, as a man of the old school *and* as hard-to-get weekend help. After serving him, Joe sank down at the other end of the table with a cup of coffee. What he really wanted was a cold beer. "How's everything at the monastery, Father?"

"About the same," said Father Otto, and helped himself to the strawberry preserves. He praised the brand, Smucker's. He said he preferred strawberry to red raspberry, and red to black raspberry, as a rule, and didn't care for the monastery stuff, as the nuns skimped on the natural ingredients. "And make too much plum."

"That so?" said Joe. He'd heard it all before. As a rule, he didn't sit with Father Otto at breakfast.

"My, but those were fine berries," said Father Otto, referring, as he had before, to some strawberries no longer grown at the monastery. "Small, yes, but with a most delicate flavor. And then Brother, he went and dug 'em out."

"Brother Gardener?" said Joe, as if in some doubt.

Father Otto, carried away by anger, could only reply by nodding.

"More toast, Father?"

"All right." Father Otto helped himself to more preserves. He kept getting ahead of himself—always more preserves than toast.

Joe produced another slice from the kitchen, and also the coffeepot. "Warm that up for you?"

"All right." But first Father Otto drained his cup. "You make good coffee here."

Joe poured, sat down again, considering what he had to say. (On his last trip to the kitchen, he had removed his apron as a hint to Father Otto that the dining room was closing.) "Father, I was thinking"— and Joe had been thinking, for the past month, ever since Bill moved in—"you *could* go back on the one-thirty bus."

Father Otto, who ordinarily returned to the monastery on the six-thirty bus, gazed away, masticating, sheeplike. He seemed to be saying that there ought to be a reason for such a drastic and sudden change in his routine.

"Know you want to get back as soon as possible," Joe said. Monks, he'd often been told (by monks), are never very happy away from their monastery. Between them and their real estate, there is a body-and-soul relationship, a strange bond. Monks are the homeowners, the solid citizens, of the ecclesiastical establishment. Other varieties of religious, and even secular priests like Joe— although he'd built a school, a convent, and now a rectory—are hoboes by comparison. That was certainly the impression you got if you spent any time with monks. So, really, what Joe was suggesting—that Father Otto return to his monastery a few hours earlier than usual—wasn't so bad, was it? "Of course, it's up to you, Father."

Father Otto folded his napkin, though it was headed for the laundry, and then he rolled it. He seemed to be looking for his napkin ring, and then he seemed to remember it was at the monastery. "All right," he said.

Bill barged in, saying, "That was Potter on the phone. Looks like there'll be one more, Father."

Seeing that he had no choice, Joe informed Father Otto that a couple of Bill's friends—classmates—were coming to dinner, and that Mrs. Pelissier, the housekeeper, would report at three. "She's been having car trouble," he added, hoping, he guessed, to change the subject, but it was no good.

"Who else is coming?" Father Otto said to Bill.

"Name's Conklin. Classmate. Ex-classmate."

Joe didn't like the sound of it. "Dropout?"

Bill observed a moment of silence. "None of us knew why Conk left. I don't think *Conk* did—at the time."

"That's often the case, Bill. It's nothing to be ashamed of," said Father Otto, looking at Joe.

"Who said it was?" Joe inquired, and then continued with Bill. "So now he's married. Right?"

"No. Not exactly."

Joe waited for clarification.

"I guess he thinks about it," Bill said.

Father Otto nodded. "We all do."

"That so?" said Joe.

Father Otto nodded. "It's nothing to be ashamed of."

"That so?" said Joe.

"Is it all right, then?" Bill said.

Joe looked at Bill intently. "Is *what* all right?"

"For Conk to come? He's a pretty lonely guy."

Father Otto was nodding away, apparently giving *his* permission.

"It's your party," Joe said, and rose from the table in an energetic manner, as a hint to Father Otto. "I'd ask you to stay for it, Father. Or Bill would—it's his party. But we plan to sit down—or stand up, it's buffet—around five. You'd have to eat and run." And somebody —Joe—would have to drive Father Otto to the bus.

"But stay if you like," Bill said.

"All right," said Father Otto.

Joe and Father Otto were watching the Twins game and drinking beer in the pastor's study when Bill brought in his friends and introduced them. The heavy one wearing a collar, which showed that he, or his pastor, was still holding the line, was Hennessy. The exhibitionist in the faded Brahms T-shirt was Potter. And the other one, the one with the mustache, a nasty affair, was Conklin.

"What's the score?" Bill asked, as if he cared.

"Four to one," Joe said.

"Twins?"

"No."

Potter and Conklin moved off to case the bookshelves, and Father Otto joined them, but Hennessy stood by, attending to the conversation.

"What inning?" Bill asked.

"Seventh"

"Who's pitching?"

Joe took a step toward the television set.

"Leave it on," Bill said. "We're going to my room for a drink."

Bill and his friends then departed, Hennessy murmuring, "See you later."

"Fine young men," said Father Otto.

"Uh-huh," Joe said. "Split a bottle, Father?"

"All right."

Joe carried the empties into the kitchen. "Everything O.K. in here?" he said to Mrs. P., and opened the refrigerator—always an embarrassing act for him, even when alone. He had cut down on snacking, though, had suffered less from "night hunger" since Bill moved in.

"Sure you want to eat in the study, Father?"

"It's Bill's party," Joe said, although he felt as Mrs. P. did about eating in the study.

"He's lucky he's got you for a pastor, Father."

"Oh, I don't know," Joe said, but didn't argue the point. He returned to the study and poured half of the beer—more than half—into Father Otto's glass. "Hey. How'd that man get on second?"

Father Otto observed the television screen closely and nodded, as if to say yes, Joe was right, there was a man on second.

"The official scorer has ruled it a single and an error, not a double," said the announcer.

"Who made the error?" Joe said, more to the announcer than to Father Otto.

"According to our records, that's the first error Tony's made this season," said the announcer.

Father Otto got up and, as was his habit from time to time, left the room.

After a bit, Joe went to see if anything was wrong, but Father Otto, who used the lavatory off the guest room, wasn't there. Then, listening in the hallway, Joe heard the old monk's voice among the others in Bill's room, and returned to the study. Sitting there alone, finishing off Father Otto's beer, Joe asked himself, What's wrong with this picture? Nothing, really, he told himself. The curate was entertaining in his room so as not to interfere with the game, the visiting priest was a fair-weather fan, if that, and so, really, nothing was wrong—it meant nothing, nothing personal that the pastor sat alone. He didn't like it, though.

One of the best things about the priesthood, Joe had been told in the seminary, is other priests—"priestly fellowship." The words had sounded corny at the time, but Joe had believed in the idea behind them and he still did. For years, though, he hadn't had room in his life for those who should now be his intimates—two of his classmates had died, and others seemed equally remote. Pursuing his building program as he had, he had been forced to associate almost exclusively with the laity, and now, at forty-four, he found he wanted more from life. And for some reason he wasn't finding as much priestly fellowship as he'd hoped to find where he kept looking for it—under his own roof.

Despite the age gap, Joe had tried hard with Father Otto. In the beginning, there had been pro football games (spoiled by Father Otto's totally uninformed comments and rather amused attitude), drives into the countryside to see the autumn foliage ("You should see it at the monastery"), visits to new churches of all denominations, since Joe would have to build a new church someday (visits discontinued because Father Otto wasn't, as he put it, terribly interested in new churches, or, for that matter, old ones, and disliked the bucket seats in Joe's car). Now, as a rule, they spent Sunday afternoon at home, in the pastor's study, sent out for seafood dinners, which Father Otto seemed to look forward to, and watched television, which the monk didn't have in his cell in the monastery. This was all right when there was something on, by which Joe meant major sports, not water-skiing, and also things like *Meet the Press* and *Face the Nation*, but Father Otto wasn't so discriminating—he enjoyed quiz programs and government propaganda. At such times, Joe would go downstairs to his office to read, or slip into his bedroom for a nap. All in all, not an ideal situation.

With Bill, Joe had tried harder, since so much more was at stake—the pastor-curate relationship. It had begun badly. Bill, reporting for duty on his first day, a Saturday, had barely made it in time for afternoon confessions, had dined out the next day without giving sufficient notice, had come in late that night, and had to be summoned to the office area the next morning. (Evidently, he'd thought that a priest just sat around in his room waiting for something to turn up.) And he'd been ordained without even a hunt-and-peck command of typing—a great blow to Joe, who'd said that a man who couldn't type was as ill-equipped for modern parish life as a man who couldn't drive, and Bill had laughed. A very bad time in the relationship.

Joe was still carrying the work load he had carried before, doing all the parish accounts and correspondence and trying to find jobs that Bill could do—quite a job itself. The future looked better, though, with Bill going ahead in his typing, using the text and records provided by Joe and his own phonograph, which, at first, at the end of each day, he'd lugged up to his room to play folk and protest songs on but now, thank God, left in his office. Bill was sweating it out now, yes, but so was Joe, and really Bill couldn't complain. It wasn't all business in the office area. With the connecting door open, they could carry on conversations desk to desk, and if the flow was rather more one way than the other, that was because there was so much that Bill didn't know about procedure and policy, about the local community, about the world in general. Here, too, Joe tried to help Bill, working from a dozen or so periodicals that crossed his desk, passing them on with some articles marked "Read" or "Skip." It was all right if Bill read the recommended matter during office hours as long as his typing and filing didn't suffer. Sometimes, too, Joe would drop in on Bill and smoke a baby cigar with him (wanted to get Bill off cigarettes), and two or three times a week, an hour before closing time, Joe would put on his hat and say, in the gruff voice he affected when he was about to be more than ordinarily decent, "Knock it off." Bill would then cover his typewriter (Joe was strict about that), and they'd go off in Joe's car, the radio playing for Bill. They had visited a number of rectories on business that could've been handled by telephone simply because Joe liked being seen with his curate. At least once a week, after what might have started out as a routine stop at the hospital or the garage (Joe's car was a lemon), they'd dined out in style, and gone on to box seats at the stadium. They had attended a half-dozen games before Joe really accepted the fact that Bill wasn't terribly interested in baseball. At Bill's suggestion, they had taken in a couple of lousy foreign movies. But mostly they spent their evenings at home, in the pastor's study, pastor in his chair, his Barcalounger, feet up, curate in attendance, with cigars and drinks (served from the bathroom, where the liquor was kept in the same drawer with the shoe polish and thus kept in its place), TV if wanted, and good talk.

Well, fairly good talk.

Little interest was shown when Joe spoke of the remarkable personalities who had flourished at the seminary during his era, and likewise when Bill spoke of his recent trials there—of piddling causes that already sounded like ancient history. Bill could say the usual things about the late Pope John, and about the present Pope, but he couldn't discuss Frank Sinatra ("the Guv'nor") or Senator Dirksen, and he hadn't even heard of people like Fishbait Miller and Nancy Dickerson. Large,

fertile areas of conversation—Capitol Hill, show business, sports—had therefore been abandoned. But what
made the likeliest subjects impossible—the difference
between Joe and Bill—was what kept them going when
they got onto religion.

Bill talked up the changes in the liturgy, the ver-
nacular, lay participation, ecumenism, and so on, and
Joe didn't. Bill claimed that religion had hit bottom in
our time and had no place to go but up, and Joe questioned both statements. Bill said that religion (though
not perhaps as we know it) was the coming thing, and
that the clergy (though not perhaps as we know them)
were the coming men. "Fuzzy thinking, Pollyanna stuff,"
said Joe, and advised Bill to stop reading Teilhard de
Chardin and other unpronounceables. So Bill was inclined to be bullish, and Joe bearish, about the future.

As for the present, the immediate present, Joe could
understand how Bill might be unhappy in his work,
considering the satisfactions there were, or were said to
be, in the priesthood, which, unfortunately, was not
what it was cracked up to be in the seminary and not
what *you* chose to make it. If Bill had expectd to labor
in certain parts of the vineyard, and not in others—in
the slums, and not in the suburbs—he should have said
so years ago and saved the diocese the expense of edu-
cating him. And if Bill felt, as he said, thwarted and
useless where he was—well, that was exactly how men
in slum parishes felt. The truth was Bill had got what
he wanted—a tough assignment—without the romantic
prop: that went with a slum parish: bums, pigeons, and
so on. Naturally, after living in the rarefied atmosphere
of the seminary, Bill was finding it hard to adjust to
reality. A slight case of the bends. That was all. Or was
it?

Sometimes, late at night, Joe would call Bill an
apostolic snob—accuse him of looking down his nose at

the parishioners just because they weren't derelicts or great sinners—and sometimes, late at night, Joe would call Bill a dreamer. In that connection, Joe had noticed that Bill had a faraway look in his eyes, and that Bill had a head like a violin. Dreamers hadn't been so common in the Church back when he'd been one himself, hadn't constituted a working majority then, Joe was saying one night, when a picture of Rudolf Hess appeared on television and Joe noticed that Hess had a head like a violin. Joe was beginning to develop his thesis, saying the fact that Hess had flown to Scotland in the hope of stopping the war, a war that still had years to run, certainly proved that he was a dreamer, when Bill interrupted: "The fact that you've got a head like a banjo, Father—what's *that* prove?" Well, Joe had tried not to show it, had smiled, but he had been hurt—a very bad moment in the relationship.

On the whole, though, they were getting along. There were nights, yes, when Bill had to be called more than once before he came out of his room, before he left off strumming his Spanish guitar, listening to FM, or talking to his friends on the phone. There were nights, too, when Bill returned to his room earlier than Joe would have liked, when Joe had maybe had one too many. . . . The truth was these weren't the nights that Joe had looked forward to during his years as a pastor without a curate, and during his years as a curate with a pastor who avoided him . . . and still they weren't bad nights, by rectory standards these days. There had been some fairly good talk—arguments, really, ending sometimes with one man making a final point outside the other man's door, or, after they'd both gone to bed, over the phone. "Bill? Joe." And there had been moments, a few, when the manifest differences of age, position, and opinion between pastor and curate had just disappeared, when Joe and Bill had entered that rather exalted and somewhat relaxed state, induced in part perhaps by drink, that Joe recognized as priestly fellowship.

At one such moment, feeling content but wondering if he couldn't do better, Joe had invited Bill to have a friend or two in for a meal sometime.

"Should I call the others, Father?" said Mrs. P., sounding apprehensive, for the others were getting kind of loud in Bill's room.

"I'll do it," Joe said, but when he saw himself knocking at Bill's door, looking in on a scene he'd been more or less excluded from, he phoned over. "*Bill?*" Either Bill or Father Otto should've answered the phone—possibly Hennessy or Potter, but *not* Conklin.

They arrived in the study like conventioneers, some carrying glasses, and immediately formed a circle that did not include Joe. He came between them, mentioning Father Otto's bus, and bumped them over to the food. Then he went and stood at the other end of the table, by the wine—ready to pour, hoping to get into conversation with someone. Father Otto was first in line. "Just like the monastery," Joe said, referring to the nice display of food on Father Otto's plate.

"Yes," said Father Otto, who'd been saying (to Hennessy) that some days were somewhat better than others to visit the monastery if one intended to eat there. "We have a cafeteria now."

"Wine, Father?"

"What kind is it?"

Joe, speaking through his nose, named the wine.

"On second thought, no," said Father Otto, and moved off with his plate, which he carefully held in both hands but in a sloping manner.

Hennessy was next, and he also refused wine. But he

complimented Joe on his building program, calling the new rectory "a crackerjack," which suggested to Joe that the works of Father Finn—*Tom Playfair, Claude Lightfoot,* and the rest—were still being read and might have figured in Hennessy's vocation, as they had in his own.

"You should see the office area," Joe said to Hennessy. "Maybe, if there's time later, I could take you around the plant."

"Oh, *no!*" said Conklin, next in line, and then turned to Potter to see if he'd heard, but Potter was talking to Bill, and Hennessy ("Maybe later, Father") was moving off, and so Conklin, after more or less insulting Joe, had to face him alone.

"Wine, Mr. Conklin?"

"*Sí, señor.*"

It went with the mustache, Joe guessed, wondering whether a priest should be addressed as "*señor,*" whether "*reverendissimo*" or something wouldn't be more like it, whether, in fact, Conklin had meant to pay him back for the "mister." At the seminary, as Conklin would know, there were still a few reverend fathers who made much of "mister," hissing it, using it to draw the line between miserable you and glorious them. That hadn't been Joe's intention. What *was* Conklin now, and what was he ever likely to be, but "mister"? It didn't pay for someone in Conklin's position to be too sensitive, Joe thought.

And listened to Potter, who was saying (to Bill) that he'd had a raw egg on his steak tartare in München and enjoyed it. " '*Mit Ei,*' they call it there."

"You can enjoy it *here,*" Joe said. "Mrs. Pelissier!" he cried, not pronouncing the housekeeper's name as he usually did, but giving it everything it had, which was plenty, in French.

Joe and everybody (except Father Otto) urged Potter to have a raw egg on his steak tartare, as in München—*Mit Ei! Mit Ei!* But Potter wouldn't do it, although Mrs. P. produced a dozen nice fresh ones, entering the study in triumph, leaving it in sorrow. Joe almost had one himself, for her sake. Potter came out of it badly.

Joe was hoping the Barcalounger would clear when he set forth with glass and plate, but Conklin was in it, and it didn't, and so he went and sat near Hennessy and Father Otto. "Never cared for buffet," he told them, and got no response. (Hennessy was saying that the monastic life was beyond one of his modest spiritual means, Father Otto that one never knew until one tried.) Joe tried the other conversation. (Potter was building up the laity, at the expense of the clergy, as was the practice of the clergy these days.) "Some of your best friends must be laymen," Joe said, and was alarmed to see Potter taking him seriously: that was the trouble with the men of Bill's generation—not too bright and in love with themselves, they made you want to hit them. "But what about the ones who empty their ashtrays in your parking lot?"

Potter smiled—*now* he thought Joe was kidding.

"Not much you can do," Conklin said. "Judah took possession of the hill country, but he couldn't drive out the inhabitants of the plain, because they had chariots of iron."

"That so?" said Joe, thinking, What *is* this? He tried his wine. "Not bad," he said to Potter and Bill (who still had their drinks from Bill's room), but he didn't get through to them. Potter was a talker.

"What kind is it?" said Father Otto.

Joe, speaking through his nose, named the wine.

"Grape," said Conklin, coming back from the table

with the bottle from which only he and Joe had par-
taken so far, and sitting down with it, in the Barcalounger. "Anybody else?"

"No, thanks," Joe said, and was silent for some time
—until he heard Conklin refer to Beans McQueen as
Beans. "You a friend of Father McQueen's?"

"They taught this course together, at the Institute,"
Bill said. "Scripture for the Laity."

"That so?" said Joe.

And the talk went on as before, on two fronts, without Joe, leaving him free to go over to the table for the
other bottle of wine. Hennessy wasn't having any, but
Father Otto was. "Grape, you say?" Joe served Father
Otto, and also himself, and left the bottle on the coffee
table in front of him, but beyond his reach—not that
wine, unfortified wine, was really alcoholic, not that *he*
was. He just had to watch himself. He wasn't a wine
drinker, but could see how he might have been one in
another time and place—one of those wise old abbés,
his mouth a-pucker with *Grand Cru*, his tongue tasting
like steak, solving life's problems by calling people "my
son."

Potter was telling Bill and Conklin that the clergy
should cast off their medieval trappings, immerse themselves in the profane everyday world, and thus reveal its
sacred character.

"That why you're immersed in that shirt?" said Joe,
but Potter just smiled and went on as before. It was odd
the way Bill looked up to Potter, odder still the way
they both looked up to Conklin—as *what*, a layman? It
was a crazy world. Father Otto was telling Hennessy
that the monastery should employ trained lay personnel
in key positions, replace the kitchen, if not the laundry,
nuns, and also certain brothers. "So Brother Gardener
has to go?" said Joe.

Father Otto turned on Joe. "*You,*" he said, speaking with deliberation, as if the wine, and whatever he'd had in Bill's room, and the beer before that, had suddenly gone to his head. "*You. Covered. Up. Those. Flowers.*"

"Flowers?" said Joe, and listened to the silence in the study. For the first time since the party began, he felt that others were interested in what he might have to say. "Things like petunias," he said, and started to tell them about the leftover sod. At once he saw that they already knew about it, that it was later than he'd thought, that he was not to escape the pastor's fate, was already being discussed in his own rectory and therefore in others by curates and visiting priests, those natural allies. "Didn't realize you felt that way about petunias, Father. Strawberries, yes."

"Humph," said Father Otto.

"Excuse me," Joe said, feeling that everybody was against him, and went over to the table, where he had work to do. He had to fire up the chafing dish, pour the juice from the pitted Bing cherries into the top pan, or blazer, place it directly over the flame, bring the juice to a boil, thicken with ½ tsp. of arrowroot dissolved in a little cold water, but Potter was telling the others that family life was in such tough shape today because Our Lord had been a bachelor, and so, carrying a dead match to the ashtray, Joe appeared among them again, saying, "We used to ask a lot of silly questions in the sem. Would Our Lord be a smoker, drive a late-model car, and so on. Kid stuff—nobody got hurt. But I wonder about some of the stuff I hear today."

"People living normal lives can't identify with Our Lord," Potter said. "Or with *us*—because of the celibacy barrier."

"That so?" said Joe. "And where you *don't* have that barrier? I mean how well do *we* identify with Our

Lord?" Joe put the question to Bill and Hennessy, too, with his eyes, passed over Conklin, tried but failed with Father Otto, who was spearing kernels of corn with his fork, making a clicking noise on his plate—rather annoying, since it broke what otherwise would have been an impressive silence.

"He's got you, Pot," said Conklin, and then to Joe: "We may be closer than I thought."

Joe, not seeing why Conklin's last words should cause Bill and Potter to look so sad, continued, "And when you consider we work at it full time, unlike the laity—well, it makes you wonder, doesn't it?"

"It did me," said Conklin

Bill sighed, and Potter held out his glass to Conklin for wine—a highball glass with ice in it. Joe said nothing about a proper glass, afraid that Potter (who'd said earlier that he longed for the day when he'd be able to say Mass with a beer mug, a coffee cup, a small flower vase of simple design, because such things were cheap and honest and made, like us, of clay) would refuse a proper glass and, furthermore, would say *why*. In that way, Potter could easily evade the issue he'd raised, the celibacy issue, as he had the egg. Potter was tricky, had to be watched, but Joe was doing that—and then Father Otto had to butt in.

"There's been a lot of talk in the community about family life, but whatever the future holds for you fellas, I think it's safe to say our status, or situation—some would say our lot—won't change. When you get right down to it, a monastery's no place for a family man."

"I'll buy that," said Joe.

"Oh, well," said Father Otto. "The community's family enough for me."

And that, Joe thought, is why you're here.

"When you get right down to it," said Conklin (to

Father Otto), "a monastery's no place for *you*. Priests weren't meant to be monks, and monks weren't meant to be priests—and *weren't* in the Age of Faith."

"We all know that," Joe said—Conklin sounded just like an ex-seminarian, or an educated layman.

"Times change," said Father Otto.

"Status-seeking," said Conklin.

Joe gave Bill a look for grinning, and to make it absolutely clear where his sympathies lay, as between Conklin and Father Otto, who appeared to be slightly wounded, Joe fetched the bottle. "Father?"

"All right," said Father Otto.

Joe filled the monk's glass, also his own, and went back to the table, with Potter's voice following him. "Why put such a premium on celibacy—on sex, really? Think of the problems it creates."

"Think of the problems it *doesn't* create," said Joe, and while Potter and the others were thinking of those problems (Joe hoped), he poured the juice from the pitted Bing cherries into the top pan, or blazer. That done, he appeared among them again, saying, "The premium isn't on sex. It isn't on celibacy. It's on efficiency and sanctity."

"Oh, *no!*" said Conklin.

"Oh, *yes*," said Joe. "Even if we don't hear much about that aspect of the priesthood today." And, having given them more food for thought, Joe left them again, for he still had work to do, but before he reached the table the impressive silence his words had produced was cruelly violated.

"*Father, how can we make sanctity as attractive as sex to the common man?*"

Joe had put that question to a Discalced Carmelite before an S.R.O. audience at the seminary during the war years, and Joe could hear it yet, that famous question, and had to expect to hear it yet from certain men

—Potter's permissive pastor was one—of that era, but *not,* Joe thought, from somebody like Conklin, and showed it.

"Got to talkin' . . . in Bill's room," Father Otto said, apologetically, and paused to watch his plate (which he'd been holding in a sloping manner) start down his outstretched leg, jump, and land on the floor, right side up. Once, twice, he nodded, as if to say no harm done, but his head hung down, finally, in an uncompleted nod.

Joe sprang into action. Others, nearer to Father Otto, had already sprung. But it was Joe who removed the fork (in the circumstances, a dangerous instrument) from Father Otto's hand and thrust it at Potter, who hesitated to take it by the greasy end, and it was Joe who deftly kicked the plate aside and told Bill to pick it up, and Joe who instructed Hennessy and Conklin, instead of foolishly trying to firm him up, to lay the monk out on the couch. Joe then changed his mind about that, in view of the sepulchral effect it might have on the party. "Bedroom! Bedroom!" he cried. "Not mine! Not mine!" Conklin and Hennessy, frog-marching Father Otto this way and that, didn't seem to know what they were doing. Then Joe saw what the trouble was. It was Conklin. Why, when there were plenty of clergy present, when the person in distress was himself one of them, why should a layman be playing such an important part? "Here, let *me,*" Joe said, shouldering in, but the layman wouldn't let go. Joe ended up with Hennessy's portion of Father Otto. And so, borne up by Joe and Conklin, the helpless monk was removed from the scene.

When Joe got back from the guest room, he found that the juice, which he had yet to thicken with ½ tsp. of arrowroot dissolved in a little cold water, had already thickened, having been kept at, rather than brought to, a boil. Until then, he had hoped to serve cherries jubilee for dessert and to do the job himself, so Mrs. P. wouldn't have to be present, but now he didn't know. The juice had definitely lost its liquidity, was hardening or charring at the edges of the top pan, or blazer. To go ahead now, with or without the arrowroot, might be a mistake. So, playing it safe, he blew out the flame, dished up the cherries as they were, room temperature and rather dry without their juice, and served them swiftly, with spoons. He said nothing, and nothing was said.

The conversation died when Joe sat down with his dish and spoon. He had tuned in earlier, though, while serving, and was curious to know why Hennessy thought that Conklin shouldn't go on teaching at the Institute. "If he's reasonably competent, and if Beans wants him back—well, why not?" said Joe, feeling broad-minded. (Hennessy, too, had that effect on him.) No response. "O.K. I'll put it another way. What if he shaved off his mustache?"

Potter and Bill shuffled their feet and protested, but Joe ignored them. "Why not?" he asked, speaking directly to Conklin.

"You talkin' about the mustache or the Institute?"

"Both."

Potter and Bill protested again.

"It's a fair question," said Conklin. "About the Institute. You better tell him, Bill"

Joe looked at Bill. "Well?"

"Conk's lost his faith," Bill said.

"That so?" said Joe. He was sorry to hear it, of course, and felt that more was expected of him, but he also felt that condolences weren't in order, since some people regarded the loss of their faith as a step forward, and since he didn't want to sound like he was rolling in the stuff himself. He now saw why Conklin had been invited, saw why so much was being made of him by Potter and Bill, saw what was really going on. It was an old-fashioned spiritual snipe hunt, such as they'd all read about, with Potter and Bill, if not Hennessy, happy to be participating, and also, it seemed, the snipe. That was the odd part.

"Conk just doesn't take God for granted—unlike some of us in the Church," Potter said, apparently to Joe. "That's been our trouble all along. Atheism and faith—true faith—have that in common. They don't take God for granted."

Joe looked cross-eyed at Hennessy.

"But Conk's not an atheist," Bill said to Joe. "Are you, Conk?"

Conklin smiled. "No, but I'm working on it."

Joe wanted to hit him.

"That's what I like about Conk," Potter said, grimly. "He's honest."

Bill nodded, grimly.

Joe sniffed. "What I don't get," he said to Conklin, "is why you want to go on teaching at the Institute if you've lost your faith. Just want to keep your hand in, or what?"

"Don't blame *Conk*," Potter said

"*Conk* wants to quit," Bill said.

"He should," Joe said, and gave him an encouraging nod.

"*No!*" cried Potter, and stood up. "What matters in teaching is a man's competence, not his private beliefs, or lack of same. And that applies to things like Scripture and theology, if they're teachable, and *I* say they are. By agnostics, infidels, and apostates, you say? *Yes!* I say. And, thank God, some of our better institutions agree!" Potter sat down.

Bill stood up. "But how many of our *seminaries,*

Pot? How can we go on calling theology the Queen of Sciences?" Bill sat down.

"How about Beans?" said Joe, without getting up. Joe was pretty sure that Beans didn't need Conklin, was just doing an ex-seminarian a favor, letting him keep his hand in, and maybe hoping for a delayed vocation. "*He* know about this? No? Better tell him, then, so he can find somebody else, if necessary."

Potter and Bill both stood up, both preaching, and Potter, of course, prevailed, but he was repeating himself.

"Look," said Joe. "The Institute isn't one of our better institutions." Even as an adventure in adult education, which was all it claimed to be, it probably didn't rate too high. "And it wouldn't be one of our better institutions if you guys pulled this off."

"It'd be a start," said Potter, sitting down.

"It'd be a stunt," said Joe, getting up. Going to the door, he took the tray from Mrs P., but on his return, with his mind on the trouble there could be over Conklin at the Institute—factions, resolutions, resignations, and so on—he overran the coffee table, jarring it and cracking his shin. In some pain, he backed up and put down the tray, saying, "I worry about you guys." Pouring and handing around coffee, sloshing it, he spoke to them as he sometimes did to Bill alone, late at night.

Home Truths

He said that he, at their age, had dearly wanted to be a saint, had trained for it—plenty of prayer and fasting, no smoking, no booze ("Actually, I didn't drink anything but beer then"), and had worn a hair shirt for a short period. At their age, *he* had worked out on himself, not on other people, and that was the difference between the men of his generation and theirs. One of the differences. "You guys even *want* to be saints? I doubt it. You're too busy with your public relations."

Changing Standards

There might be worlds to be won, souls to be harvested, and so on, but not with stunts and gimmicks. He had been rather pessimistic about the various attempts to improve the Church's image, and he had been right. Vocations, conversions, communions, confessions, contributions, general attendance, all down. And why not? "We used to stand out in the crowd. We had quality control. We were the higher-priced spread. No more. Now if somebody drops the ball somebody else throws it into the stands, and that's how we clear the bases. Tell the man in the next parish that you fornicated a hundred and thirty-six times since your last confession, which was one month ago, and he says, 'Did you think ill of your fellow-man?' It's a crazy world."

Stranded

There had always been a shortage of goodness in the world, and evil and ignorance were still facts of life, but where was the old intelligence? He had begun to wonder, as he never had before, about the doctrine of free will. People, he feared, might not be able to exercise free will any more, owing to the decline in human intelligence. How else explain the state of the country, and the world, today? "We don't, maybe we *can't*, make the right moves—like those poor whales you read about. We're stranded."

Human Nature

The Church was irrelevant today, not concerned enough with the everyday problems of war, poverty, segregation, and so on, people said, but such talk was itself irrelevant, was really a criticism of human nature. Sell what you have and follow me, Our Lord had told the rich young man—who had then gone away sad. That was human nature for you, and it hadn't changed. Let him take it who can, Our Lord had said of celibacy —and few could take it, then or now. "And that applies to heroic sacrifice of all kinds. Let's face it."

Bruegel the Elder

People, most people, lay *and* clerical, just weren't up to much. Liturgists, of course, were trying to capitalize on that fact, introducing new forms of worship, reviving old ones, and so on, but an easy way would never be found to make gold out of lead. Otherwise the saints and martyrs would have lived as they had, and died, in vain. All this talk of community, communicating, and so on—it was just whistling in the dark. "Life's not a cook-out by Bruegel the Elder and people know it."

Too Far?

Sure it was a time of crisis, upheaval, and so on, but a man could still do his job. The greatest job in the world, divinely instituted and so on, was that of the priest, and yet it was still a job—a marrying, burying, sacrific-ing job, plus whatever good could be done on the side. It was *not* a crusade. Turn it into one, as some guys were trying to do, and you asked too much of it, of yourself, and of ordinary people, invited nervous break-downs all around. Trying to do too much was something the Church had always avoided, at least until recently. At the Council, the so-called conservatives—a perse-cuted minority group if ever there was one—had only been afraid of going too far too soon, of throwing the baby out with the bath water. "And rightly so."

Flying Saucers

The Church couldn't respond to all the demands of the moment or she'd go the way of those numerous sects that owed their brief existence to such demands. People had to realize that what they wanted might not be what they needed, and if they couldn't—well, they couldn't. Religion was a weak force today, owing to the decline of human intelligence. It was now easy to see how the Church, though she'd endure to the end, as promised by Our Lord, would become a mere remnant of herself. In the meantime, though, the priest had to get on with his job, *such as it was*. As for feeling thwarted and useless, he knew that feeling, but he also knew what it meant. It meant that he was in touch with reality, and that was something these days. Frequently reported, of course, like flying saucers, were parishes where priests and people were doing great things together. "But I've never seen one myself, if it's any consolation to you guys," Joe said, and paused.

Did the impressive silence mean that they were now seeing themselves and their situations in a new light, in the clear north light of reality? Bill, *finally*? Potter? Even Conklin? Joe hoped so, in all cases. On the whole, he was satisfied with the response. The bath-water bit hadn't gone down very well (groans from Potter, "Oh, *no!*" from Conklin), and there had been other interruptions, but Joe had kept going, had boxed on, opening cuts, closing eyes, and everybody, including Conklin, looked better to him now.

He wanted Hennessy and Potter to come out again,

and not just to visit Bill, and not just to discuss their problems with him (Joe), though that would be all right. He wanted them to come out whenever they felt like it, whenever they needed a lift, a little priestly fellowship. Actually, there might be more for them with him, and more for him with them, than with Bill—who, to tell the truth, wasn't much fun. It could happen, first Hennessy and Potter coming, then coming with others, and these in turn with others. There would be nights, perhaps, when Bill wouldn't leave his room. "Where's Bill?" "Oh, he's listening to FM." Joe's rectory could become a hangout for the younger clergy, a place where they'd always be sure of a drink, a cigar, and if he put a table in the living room, never used now, a cue. Pastors at first critical ("Stay the hell away from there!") would sing his praises ("He sure straightened out that kid of mine"). Time marching on, Hennessy seldom seen, a bishop somewhere, first of the old crowd to make it, but the others still around, pastors now with curates of their own—tired, wiser men, the age gap narrowing between them and their old mentor, not so old, really, and in excellent health, eating and drinking less. A few missing, yes, the others, though, still coming out to Joe's—in a crazy world, an asylum of sanity—for priestly fellowship, among them, perhaps, Father Conklin, old Conk, a pretty lonely guy for a while there, until he started coming out, shaved off his mustache, found his lost faith, the road back, second spring, and so on.

"So what's the answer?" said Potter. "Watch the Twins?"

"Those bores," said Conklin.

Hennessy reproved them with a look, and spoke with his future authority. "What's the answer, Father?"

Eying Father Otto's glass on the coffee table, Joe said, "A few monks saved civilization once. Could be the answer again. Principle's sound. You'd have to work out the details. Wouldn't have to be monks. Could happen right here." Joe reached for Father Otto's glass, the last of the wine, and swirled it clockwise, counterclockwise, clockwise, denying himself before downing it. "Wanna see how Father is," he said then. "Be right back." At the door, as he was about to leave them, he turned and said, "How can we make sanctity as attractive as sex? Answer I got was 'Just have to keep trying.' Not much of an answer. Nobody remembers it—just the question. Guess it's the answer to all these questions. Be right back."

Father Otto's eyes opened when Joe approached the bed. "Get you anything, Father?" Joe asked.

"All right."

"Aspirin?"

"All right."

Joe administered aspirin and water to Father Otto, flipped his pillow, eased him down. "Want your shoes off?"

"Is the party over?"

"Not yet."

"Then why is everybody leaving?" said Father Otto, his eyes closing.

"Not yet," Joe said patiently, but when he returned to the study he saw that he was wrong.

Hennessy—he was the only one there—said, "How is he?"

"All right," Joe said.

Led by voices to a window on the street side, gazing down, he saw Bill, Potter, and Conklin talking to a young woman—older than they were, though—in a convertible.

"Conklin had to leave," Hennessy said.

Joe came away from the window. "So I see."

"Want to thank you, Father."

"It was Bill's party."

"All the same." Hennessy seemed to know what it was like to be a pastor. "Oh, and I should thank the housekeeper."

"Good idea." Joe saw Hennessy, who'd go far, off to the kitchen, and returned to the window. Below, the young woman moved over on the seat and the mustache took the wheel. Potter and Bill then fell all over themselves saying goodbye, making it look hard to do. And the convertible drove away. Then, to Joe's surprise—he had meant to say something about coming out again, soon—Hennessy appeared below, having, it seemed, left the rectory by the back door. Without a word or sign to Potter and Bill, who stood together, Hennessy got into the driver's seat of the black sedan at the curb. Potter and Bill then parted, rather solemnly, Joe thought, and Potter got into the *back* seat of the black sedan. It drove away. And a few moments later Bill entered the study.

"Who was that?" Joe asked.

"His mistress."

Joe stared at Bill. "Say that again."

Bill said it again.

"*That* what he calls her? How d'ya know *that*?"

"He told us."

"He did, huh?" Joe was thinking if he had a mistress he wouldn't tell everybody.

"He's honest about it, Father. You have to give him credit for that."

"I do, huh?"

Father Otto came in, looking much the same.

"You missed your bus," Joe said, and then to Bill, "Why don't they get married?"

"Complications."

"Like what?"

"She's already married."

Joe sniffed. "Great."

"Her husband won't give her a divorce. *He's* still a Catholic."

"Say that again."

Bill said it again.

Joe turned away. "And you wanna get back to your monastery—right?"

"How?" said Father Otto.

"I'll drive you."

"Eighty miles?" said Bill. "Can't he stay overnight?"

"He wants to get back to his monastery. I need the air. Well, what d'ya say, Father?"

"All right," said Father Otto.

FAREWELL

In July, about a month before he was to retire, the Bishop of Ostergothenburg (Minnesota), through a clerical error, received a letter from the Chancery, his own office, asking the clergy of the diocese to contribute—pastors twenty dollars, assistants ten dollars—toward buying him a car.

The Bishop was unhappy about the letter. Why set a goal that might not be attained? Why be so explicit about the nature of the proposed farewell gift? Wouldn't men driving old clunks be put off? Why not just say "gift," or "suitable gift"? And, since he'd still be there, living upstairs in the brownstone mansion that was also the Chancery office, why say farewell? Arguing with the letter in this fashion, and wondering about the response to it, and hearing nothing, the Bishop spent his last days on the throne in a state of apprehension.

The day before he retired—he'd still heard nothing —he gave the girl in the office his set of keys to the aging black Cadillac that belonged to the diocese and was what he'd driven when he drove, which had been seldom.

The day after he retired (he'd still heard nothing), he went out and bought himself a car, a Mercedes—a grey one, as there wasn't a black one in stock. When his successor, Bishop Gau, saw it, he said, "Bishop, *we* were giving you a car. The clergy. I sent out a letter. I was just waiting until I heard from everybody."

"You should live so long," said the Bishop, embarrassed, certain that the response had been disappointing, if only because of the tone of the letter.

But when presented with what Bishop Gau smilingly called "the loot," which included a check from him for a hundred dollars and one from his chum Father Rapp for fifty dollars, the Bishop reckoned that it was only a few hundred less than it might have been ideally, and that the clergy—they were a good bunch, by and large—*did* appreciate him.

In the following days, weeks, months—he was still at it in October—he wrote and thanked the contributors but returned their contributions, saying the money could be put to better use. Quite a job, writing a hundred and sixty-eight letters by hand, personalizing each without showing partiality and without repeating himself, except in promising to remember each man at the altar, asking to be so remembered himself, and signing his name, "✝ John Dullinger," or, in a few instances, simply, "✝ John."

Early in October, when all the contributors had

been taken care of (except Bishop Gau and Father Rapp) and the weather was still fine, he got out the Mercedes and drove forty-six miles to see a church under construction, the last of many he'd laid corner- stones for—his administration, so rich in achievements, will be remembered not least for its churches (Oster- gothenburg *Times*). He was home safely, before dark, very pleased with the car's performance. He took two more trips. He was planning another—in October, with the trees a riot of color, the diocese was at its best. But then it rained and froze hard, and was winter.

At that point his retirement really began.

He still said the eight o'clock Mass at what was now the ex-cathedral (the new one was inconvenient), had break- fast at the rectory there, and lunch at home—prepared by the cleaning woman, though, since his housekeeper had retired. But between the time he got back in the morning and the time he left for his evening meal at the Hotel Webb, there was now a bad eight-hour period that hadn't been there before. He read, tried to watch TV, or just sat, sometimes wishing he had an absorbing hobby or a schol- arly mind. (But how many bishops did, nowadays?) If a car drove into the parking lot below, he went to the win- dow to see who it was (too often only Bishop Gau or Father Rapp), then returned to his chair, to *Who's Who in the Midwest*, which interested him more than *Who's Who in America* (he was in both), or to the *Times*, or the diocesan paper, which he read these days with more care and less satisfaction: there was a difference between reading and being the news.

Still, he didn't exactly envy Bishop Gau, with things as they were in the country and the Church, and be- coming more so every day, though the diocese was still in pretty good shape, still heavily rural and Catholic. Bishop Gau was better suited to the times, more tolerant of the chumps coming out of the seminary, and of the older, suddenly unstable men, than the Bishop had been—running into one of them dressed in civvies, he'd say, "What's the matter, Father? Drunk, or ashamed of the priesthood?"

He could easily get carried away, which was bad even when the cause was good, and for this weakness he'd sometimes paid. Carried away, he'd written checks for a couple of hard-up dioceses behind the Iron Curtain whose bishops he'd met in Rome and liked, entertaining them and others at the Grand, where he always stayed, and then, returning home, had been humiliated by his pussyfooting consultors—thereafter all such checks had to be countersigned by the Auxiliary (as he was then). Bishop Gau, who had risen swiftly, helped by the Bishop at first, by himself and Rome later, understood finance, both high and low, better than the Bishop ever had. Bishop Gau and Father Rapp were now driving fast new Fords, identical silver ones, and the aging black Cadillac had vanished, presumably in a three-for-two deal. Bishop Gau handled such matters very well. Most matters, in fact. But he hadn't handled the Bishop's farewell gift very well.

The Bishop had been compelled, in the circumstances, to invest in an expensive car for which he had little use and then to take another loss by returning the contributions, the loot. That word, as he interpreted it, had left him no choice. But many who'd had their contributions returned to them would mention that awesome little fact, and that was where the Bishop had them, those two, Bishop Gau and Father Rapp, for he still had their checks. He often wondered what they must be thinking, and enjoyed the prospect of their hearing of his philanthropy from other contributors—a growing number. That was about all the Bishop had going for him these days.

His evening meal at the Hotel Webb had become more important to him these days, not that his appetite had increased. No, he just liked it at the Webb, where he'd always liked it, *more*: the good food there and the lighting (not dim), the tables and chairs (no booths), the background music, and, in December, the tasteful decorations and the big tree—a real one, green (un-whitewashed) and grown in the diocese. When people, other diners, paused at his table to pay their respects—they still did—he appreciated it more than he had in the past, and he wasn't so wary of those in the selling line, or of the clergy. And when told how sorry people were that he was retired he was happy to hear it, even when it reflected on his successor, as it sometimes did, at which times he praised his successor, or acted as if he hadn't heard.

That was how he acted one evening early in December when Monsignor Holstein—once rector of the Cathedral, Vicar-General of the diocese, and the Bishop's right-hand man, now only pastor of St. John Nepomuk's, New Pilsen—said, "*Wie geht's?* You're sorely missed these days, John."

The Bishop invited Monsignor Holstein to sit down, which he did, in his white socks, saying, "Like old times, John."

Again the Bishop acted as if he hadn't heard, for, while agreeing it was like old times—the two of them together again at the Webb at the corner table, where they'd so often gone into the problems of the diocese and planned the campaigns—he was also regretting his later treatment of Monsignor Holstein, who had taken it so well at the time and recently had contributed his full pastor's share toward the farewell gift. Not vindictive, a

good man in his way, Monsignor Holstein, but an ideal-
ist. Life had certainly been less difficult for the Bishop
and others, including, unfortunately, the humanists at
the normal school and the management of the Orpheum,
after the man left town. Never content to leave well
enough alone, always after the Bishop to do something
—always something—Monsignor Holstein might have
risen even higher, or stayed where he was, but for that
weakness. And it came out again that evening at the
Webb, with the cigars, when he spoke of this woman, a
Mrs. Nagel, in the country who thought she'd seen an
apparition of Our Lady in a tree on several likely occasions. Always something, yes.

Oh, the Bishop agreed that it would take something
sensational to get people thinking along more spiritual
lines these days, and that this *could* be it, and, if so, that
it would be a great thing for the diocese. But this woman's pastor, a reliable man, and this woman's husband,
also reliable, a school-bus driver—they weren't too sym-
pathetic, the Bishop understood, and that, while not
unheard of in such cases ("Those closest to the scene
are often the last to believe, John"), settled it for the
Bishop. "See the Auxiliary," he said—he still thought of
Bishop Gau as the Auxiliary—and let it stand.

"Saw him this afternoon, John."

Yes, the Bishop from his window had watched Monsignor Holstein arrive at the Chancery that afternoon.
"What'd he say?"

"Can't give credence to this woman. Too many fakes."

Yes, but if the Bishop were to visit this woman
mightn't *he* give credence to her? Monsignor Holstein
seemed to think not. A slap in the face, wasn't it? Yes,
but wasn't that what being retired was? So far, there
had been—and, yes, there would be—fewer Christmas
cards for him this year. It was the office that mattered,
and nowhere more than in the Church—which other-

wise would be just another institution and the gates of Hell would prevail against it. "The Auxiliary's right."

"*John, what if he's wrong?*"

"*He'd* still be right." The Bishop knew what he meant. "*He's* the Bishop now."

Monsignor Holstein said, "History hasn't been kind to the hierarchy in these cases, John."

Late that night, on his knees in his pajamas in the hall-way, the Bishop pushed two envelopes under the door of the Chancery office, each envelope containing a Christmas card and a check, each check annotated some months earlier (in case he died unexpectedly): "Much obliged but can be put to better use, ✝ J.D." And then he went to bed again, and this time he slept.

Traveling north the next afternoon in the Mercedes, he had no trouble until, a mile past Fahrenheit, turning off U.S. 52, he was fiercely honked at by a truck. He activated his turn signal to make amends, and drove, flashing and drumming, down a crushed-rock road a half-mile or so, coming then to a white farmhouse with an orange school bus in the driveway and, parked be-hind the bus, a car, the color of which was reassuring. With his signal still flashing, right, he turned in, left, and came to rest behind the black car.

Monsignor Holstein materialized alongside the Mer-cedes—so it seemed to the Bishop, who'd been having trouble again with his seat belt. They went around to the back of the house, Monsignor Holstein saying the front door wasn't used in cold weather, the Bishop as-sessing the Nagel property, noting the windbreak of blue spruce, the only sizable trees, though there were many seedlings.

Lest Mrs. Nagel, perhaps put up to it by Monsignor

Holstein, attempt to kiss the episcopal ring, which was a practice best confined to the clergy these days, the Bishop kept his gloves on—a needless precaution. Mrs. Nagel was more concerned with Monsignor Holstein and his glasses, which had misted over in the warm kitchen, and which she polished with a linen towel while he stood blindly by, the Bishop enjoying the scene as one who, though older, wore glasses only for reading. In Mrs. Nagel, who was blond, fairly young, fifty or so, he thought he saw the perky, useful, down-to-earth type of woman, a type he associated with hospital nuns and airline stewardesses, and liked, but he wondered that he didn't see something else in *her*.

"Now, shoo!" she said when she'd finished with the glasses, and returned to the cake she was frosting.

So the Bishop and Monsignor Holstein, both smiling —both firm believers in the supremacy of women in certain areas—left the kitchen and passed through the dining room, where, as in the kitchen, there were numerous plants, and on into the living room, where there were many more. Yes, all kinds of green, growing things (some, in tubs, were immense), and so thick that the Bishop, settling down on the settee, and Monsignor Holstein, over by the TV, which was crawling with vines, had to look through a gap in order to see each other face to face.

"What'd I tell you, John?"

"What?"

"She's a real homemaker."

"Yes." Yes, that was in Mrs. Nagel's favor, from the human standpoint. But when the Bishop thought of spiritual phenomena (of which he had no firsthand experience) he thought of way-out types. And that Mrs. Nagel wasn't one of them, that she wasn't, according to Monsignor Holstein, unusually devout—only went to Mass on Sundays and holy days of obligation, to confession once a month—that she was to all appearances just a good, average Catholic, and not some kind of nut, was not in her favor, in the Bishop's view. That, though, was what was so wonderful about this case, according to Monsignor Holstein, who, though—in interpreting it as he did, as a sign from Heaven that the traditional precepts and practices of the Church were still O.K.— might have a vested interest, the Bishop feared. Monsignor Holstein, like many pastors in recent years, had been under considerable pressure from curates, parishioners, and media, all crying change, change, change. The Bishop had been under similar pressure but could be more objective now, being retired, and the truth was he couldn't see this woman, though he'd liked her in the kitchen, as one specially chosen by Heaven.

No, and when she came into the living room and sat where he could see her, beside him on the settee, he still couldn't see her in that role. Nor could he while, over coffee and cake, they listened to her story, which was on tape because she'd had so many visitors and dreaded repeating it. ("The Little Flower felt the same way," said Monsignor Holstein.) The Bishop resented that— the Little Flower, after all, was a canonized saint of many years' standing—and after he'd heard the tape, which he also resented, believing an exception should have been made in his case, he was silent.

"Bishop, you're free to ask questions," said Monsignor Holstein, whom the Bishop, since moving over on the settee for Mrs. Nagel, could no longer see.

"Oh, am I?" said the Bishop tartly, pausing to let the words sink into the greenery where Monsignor Holstein was, and then he addressed himself to Mrs. Nagel. "This branch"—this branch that had disturbed her sleep and that she'd been about to cut off one morning when the apparition first appeared to her in that very tree, the figure of a woman all in blue, smiling but shaking her head—"has it stopped brushing against the house?"

"Oh, no. Not when the wind blows hard from the north."

The Bishop had known as much from Monsignor Holstein, but was checking, testing. "Still brushes against the house?"

"Oh, yes, when the wind blows hard from the north. But I don't mind it *now*."

"No miracles yet," Monsignor Holstein said, from his concealed position, "and none are claimed."

There were footsteps overhead. The Bishop said, "What does your husband say, Mrs. Nagel?"

"Oh, Mart never did mind it. His hearing's not so good."

There were footsteps on the stairs. The Bishop said, "I meant, what does he say about . . . all this?"

Mrs. Nagel laughed—an honest laugh, the Bishop thought, nothing bitter about it. "Oh, Mart just thinks I'm seeing things."

Monsignor Holstein said, "Those closest to the scene are often the last to believe."

"Mart just doesn't like all the visitors," said Mrs. Nagel. "Oh, he's very good. But there've been so many visitors—*busloads*—and we just don't have, you know, the facilities."

The back door slammed.

"Mart has to go for the kids," said Mrs. Nagel.

The Bishop, with an effort, got to his feet, saying, "Shouldn't we move our cars, Monsignor?"

"It's all right," said Mrs. Nagel.

"Ground's frozen," said Monsignor Holstein.

The Bishop moved over to the side window and peeked through the foliage there. He saw the bus go by on the lawn, traveling fast.

"Mart's late," said Mrs. Nagel.

The Bishop, who'd been wondering why Mr. Nagel hadn't come in to meet him, sat down, saying, "On these occasions"—so far there had been five occasions, all feast days of Our Lady, counting Christmas as one— "*she*, whoever she is, never says *who* she is?"

"No."

"And you've never asked?"

"No, I *know*."

The Bishop was silent for a moment, weighing the claims of faith against the demands of prudence, which had been his job for thirty years but hadn't got any easier. "And the message—it's always the same?"

"Yes."

"And you understand it?"

"Oh, yes."

"When did she tell you not to tell it to anybody else?"

"Oh, Father Barnett told me that."

The Bishop had known that, but again was checking, testing. "So he's the only one you've told it to?"

"And Mart. I told him before I told Father, but Father said that was all right. Just not to tell anybody else."

"You accept that from Father, do you?"

"*Oh, yes.*"

The Bishop had to smile. "Because he's your pastor and confessor?"

"Of course."

The Bishop had to smile again. "Even though he may not himself—believe?"

"Oh, yes." And Mrs. Nagel, as she had earlier at the idea that she could be seeing things, laughed.

And that was exactly how a woman chosen by Heaven would and should respond to skeptics in this world, the Bishop believed, but what impressed him even more, what really moved him, was the way this woman deferred to her doubting pastor—to proper ecclesiastical authority.

What a wonderful world this would be if everybody did the same!

"I have no more questions, Monsignor," the Bishop said.

On the way home, alone in the Mercedes, the Bishop stopped at the rectory in Fahrenheit and rang the doorbell. "Is Father in?"

"In!" cried the housekeeper.

Father Barnett, in his late fifties, the kind of priest once taken for granted and now much prized, stable, was in his bedroom, in a wingback chair, with a pillow behind him. His first words to the Bishop were "Yesterday, Bishop, going for the alarm—I keep the clock there on the TV, out of reach, so I have to get up when it rings. Anyway, *phffft*. Slipped disk. What they *call* it, but *they don't know*. I've talked to 'em in Minneapolis. I've talked to 'em in St. Paul. We had a couple of back men here from Rochester, up here fishing, and I talked to 'em. Waste of time. Some of 'em will admit it, some of 'em won't. Bishop, there are two parts of the human body we still know nothing about—the back and the head. Or next to nothing, I'd say, from talking to 'em. I've *stopped* talking to 'em, Bishop. Treat myself. A *firm* pillow, Bishop. *Not* soft. *Pressure's* what you want. Give your back support. Give your tissues a chance to heal. That's all you can do. And wait. I'll be all right in a few days, Bishop. I always am. Lucky I was able to treat it at once. Not like the last time. Was under the bed, straightening the boards—I have boards under my bed, Bishop—and couldn't make myself heard. Housekeeper out. Funny feeling, Bishop. Flat on your back, paralyzed, see your whole life pass before you, and so on. Sit down, Bishop. What brings *you* up here?"

"Mrs. Nagel."

Father Barnett nodded.

"Monsignor Holstein was there."

Father Barnett nodded.

"Strange case."

Father Barnett nodded.

"Well, we can talk about it later, Father."

The Bishop (he hadn't sat down) stepped over to the phone, dialed the Chancery and spoke to the girl in the office, said he'd be in Fahrenheit for a few days ("Father Barnett's down with his back, nothing serious"), asked that the ex-cathedral and the Webb be notified, and hung up.

Father Barnett said, "This is mighty good of you, Bishop."

The Bishop nodded.

Then he went downstairs, and after speaking to the housekeeper he drove to the business district and made a few purchases, among them an alarm clock. He was recognized by clerks in stores, and by other shoppers, farmers and their wives who knew from his pastoral letters over the years that they were his favorite people, and when he was standing out in the street with the door of the Mercedes open, about to embark, he was honked at by a woman in a passing car with one of those musical horns—all of which was personally gratifying. But, more important, it showed that the Church was well regarded locally, and, *more* important, since there was nothing special about the town (except, maybe, its nearness to Mrs. Nagel, whom one farmer's wife had mentioned), it showed that the diocese was still in good heart.

He pulled into the driveway when he returned to the rectory, and was sorry he had to leave the Mercedes

out in the cold (only a one-car garage and Father Barnett's car was in it). Rather than ring the bell again, he
entered the rectory by the back door, and, rather than
wait until the day he departed, he presented the housekeeper with a box of chocolates then, along with a carton of eggs he said "somebody" had given him, rather
than mention Mrs. Nagel. With a breviary from Father
Barnett, he went over to the church, where, after familiarizing himself with the light switches in the sacristy,
he sat in a pew and read his office until the Angelus
sounded automatically overhead, then stood. Returning
to the rectory, again using the back door, he dined
alone—not as well as he might have at the Webb but
well enough.

On a tip from the housekeeper, he dropped in on a
gathering of women in the church basement that evening, and a good thing he did, for word had got around
that he was in residence, and there was a much larger
turnout than usual, so he was told. At his insistence, the
program proceeded as planned—a talk by one of the
women on Christmas in Bethlehem—but when it was
over he was again asked to speak. So he did—on Christmas in Rome, not very well. Leaving Rome, he traced
his career in the Church, from curate to pastor to
bishop, from North Dakota to Minnesota, to the diocese
—incidentally, he said, the best place in the world to be
at Christmastime, or any other time. For this he was
warmly applauded, and should not have gone on to say
that if the history of the human race had been different
the first Christmas might have been celebrated in more
suitable surroundings, which had confused some of the
women and offended the one who'd spoken earlier. Still,
a very successful evening. Held in conversation (several
women mentioned Mrs. Nagel), he didn't get back to
the rectory until ten.

He watched the news with Father Barnett. Then

they had a drink, the able-bodied one going down to the kitchen for ice, and played cribbage—something the Bishop hadn't done since seminary. Father Barnett talked about his back and his parish, more about the former than about the latter, and didn't mention Mrs. Nagel. After an hour, the Bishop retired to his room, out nineteen dollars and very tired, but lay awake in his new pajamas, listening to his new alarm clock, which had a loud tick.

The next morning, he saw that it had snowed on the Mercedes. After Mass, borrowing a broom from the housekeeper, he swept the car and part of the walk, working up an appetite. After breakfast, he looked in on Father Barnett, who asked about the attendance at Mass in his absence, as pastors will, and when given the count, which the Bishop knew from the housekeeper was three times the usual for a weekday, just nodded, as pastors will.

The Bishop made himself useful that morning—answered the phone, saw people (only two), and had a nice talk with the mailman, as well as with the man who delivered the fuel oil. In the afternoon, the Bishop called at the jail and admonished the no-good husband of a sad case he'd seen that morning (and written a check for), after which he called at the Chrysler garage, since there wasn't a Mercedes dealer in Fahrenheit, and arranged for the car to stay there, since it had again started to snow. He ordered snow tires for his rear wheels. Then he walked over to the Rexall store, where he exchanged his alarm clock for a travel model with a quiet tick, bought a combination snow brush and ice scraper for the Mercedes, and joined the proprietor at the soda fountain in a cup of coffee. He was soon having another with the local Lutheran minister—a pleasant, if somewhat intellectual, young man—who drove him back to the rectory.

That evening, seeing lights flashing in the church basement, he went over to investigate, and there were the Scouts!

He returned to the rectory too late for the news, after a nice talk with the Scoutmaster and an Eagle (a vocation?), but not too late for a drink and cribbage. He heard more about Father Barnett's back, and still nothing about Mrs. Nagel, about whom he was now less inclined to ask. He did better at cribbage that night, losing eleven dollars, and went to bed less tired, though he'd had another busy day. For some time he lay awake, being pleased with his new clock, its quiet tick, and with himself, as he hadn't been for thirty years. It was good to be working as a parish priest again.

Three days later, the Bishop said goodbye to the housekeeper (with whom he'd had a nice talk) and to Father Barnett, who, now recovered, saw him to the front door, where (and this after repeatedly telling himself that he was retired, that it was none of his business now, that he wouldn't do this) the Bishop asked, "What about Mrs. Nagel?"

Father Barnett replied, "She's a good person, Bishop. Of her sincerity I have no doubt. But there's this that leads me to believe—*not* to believe, Bishop. This so-called message. Since it was told to me in confession, I can't tell you what it is. But I can tell you this—that it's noncontroversial, nothing about praying for the conversion of Russia, China, or the U.S., and that I advised her to keep still about it (naturally, I didn't tell her this) because it wouldn't be believed, even by people who believe in the visions, and I was afraid she'd be hurt. Should've advised her to keep still about the visions—I know that now—but doubted at the time that I could make it stick. Should've tried. Should've imposed total silence, or none at all. I fell between two stools, Bishop, and I'm the one to blame. Not Mrs. Nagel. She's a good person. Sincere. About all I can say, Bishop. There are two parts of the human body we still know nothing about."

After that, the Bishop left.

That evening, he dined at the Webb, said the eight o'clock at the ex-cathedral the next morning, and resumed his routine at home. But the following night he was in the rectory at Gebhardt, near Fahrenheit, in response to a call for help (flu), and was there for five days, including a Sunday. The day he returned home, a call came from Glanville, in the western part of the diocese, word of his availability having spread among the clergy, and he was there for twelve days (two Sundays). While there, he had a call from Grasshopper Lake (flu again), whence he proceeded directly, not returning home. He spent the days of Christmas in Grasshopper Lake, and was very happy there, nightly entertaining members of the choir in the rectory—a grand bunch, for whom he kept the beer coming and had the piano tuned. From there he went on to Pumphrey, was there ten days, and so it was the middle of January when he got back home.

"Look," Bishop Gau said, "you don't have to go on livery-horsing"—what the monks at the college, who helped out in parishes on weekends, called it—but then he spoke of the situation at Buell (with a mission at Kuhl), where the pastor, one of the few priests in the diocese not ordained by the Bishop, and one of the few noncontributors to his farewell gift, was AWOL. Bishop Gau said he thought that Father (soon to be Monsignor) Rapp, even though it was the height of the bowling season, should go to Buell temporarily, to still the waters. The Bishop, believing he'd be better in such a delicate situation—more experience and more, though he was retired, clout—said he'd go, gassed up, and went.

In Buell and Kuhl, he disposed of the amateurish posters (Peace, Joy, Love, and so on) in the churches, got the women to scrub the floors and pews, the men to wax and polish them, participating in these activities himself. He visited all the parishioners in their homes, spoke here and there, honoring all invitations, and, in general, did what he could (threw big parties in both places) to make the people forget their late pastor, except, of course, in their prayers. Owing to the special circumstances, he also said Mass daily in Kuhl, which meant driving twenty-eight miles over an unimproved road before breakfast, through ice and snow, for which, though, the Mercedes was equipped.

When, after a month, he left Buell, the car had ice on its roof (unheated garage), frozen glunk under its fenders, salt on its tires, was looking older and grayer, but was still a great performer. The Bishop couldn't say as much for himself. After a bad night at home, he checked into the hospital (flu). When he came out ten days later, he was still in demand—two calls the first day—but had to say no, he wasn't himself yet, he was convalescing.

During this period, one afternoon about three, he saw Father Barnett arrive at the Chancery and a few minutes later, in his black car, Monsignor Holstein and Mrs. Nagel.

I may be called upon, he thought, and put on his shoes, collar, and coat. Then he hovered about, waiting for the phone to ring, until he began to feel foolish doing this. So he sat down with *Who's Who in the Midwest*.

After a bit, though, the phone did ring.

The Auxiliary. "Bishop, I didn't know you'd visited Mrs. Nagel."

Not a question, and so why say anything?

"Bishop, if I'd known"—as he should have known; that was the implication beneath the apologetic tone— "I would've called you earlier."

Again, not a question.

"I just now found out, Bishop."

Not a question.

"Bishop, if you're not too busy up there, could you come down?"

"Be glad to," said the Bishop, and hurried down.

Entering the big inner office, once his own, he stopped at the first chair, expecting to be directed to another, one near the desk, but he wasn't, and so sat down, as the others did then—Bishop Gau at the desk, to his right Monsignor Rapp, and facing them Mrs. Nagel, Monsignor Holstein, Father Barnett.

"Mrs. Nagel, I appreciate it, the way you've answered my questions, especially now I know you were visited by the Bishop, here. I'm sorry I didn't know that before," said Bishop Gau (the Bishop, *in petto*, replying, *O.K., O.K.*). "And I'm sorry I had to ask you to tell your story again, but thought I should hear it live. I can understand, though, why you decided to cut a tape. Just as I can understand your husband's feelings about visitors. I don't like to say it, Mrs. Nagel, but it's possible, even for one in my position, to see too much of people. I'm sure the Bishop, here, will vouch for that."

The Bishop wasn't sure he would, but nodded to be helpful, wondering what the hell was wrong—*something* was, from the sound of it.

"Mrs. Nagel, I want this understood. A thing like this can take years, even centuries, to check out, and then what? Win or lose, it's still a matter of faith. Anyway, whatever I've said, or might say, is in no way a judgment—official, personal, or any other kind—on you or your experiences. Is that understood, Mrs. Nagel?"

"Sure."

"Good. Now, about your purpose in coming here today. While considering this, while *you* have my sympathy, Mrs. Nagel, I must also consider what, in my opinion, is best for all concerned. And then, of course, I can only advise, not command. Now, what I advise, Mrs. Nagel, is what your pastor, here, has already advised. Namely, silence. You've done very well so far."

"I know. But I don't like it this way, and I never did," Mrs. Nagel said, giving the Bishop the impression that she had said this earlier, before he came in. "Why *shouldn't* I tell people the message?"

The Bishop thought he heard somebody (Monsignor Holstein?) moan.

"People wouldn't believe you, Mrs. Nagel," said Father Barnett, sounding, the Bishop thought, *too* calm.

"*Some* people don't believe me now."

"More wouldn't," said Father Barnett. "Many more."

"I wouldn't mind. I don't mind now."

The Bishop distinctly heard Monsignor Holstein moan.

Bishop Gau said, "Mrs. Nagel, I have to consider what, in my opinion, is best for all concerned, including you. And I advise silence. Not only about the message but about everything concerning your experiences. Silence, Mrs. Nagel."

"But *why*?"

"My *dear* Mrs. Nagel," said Monsignor Holstein, and then held his jaw, which he had been holding previously.

Monsignor Rapp cleared his throat in such a way as to attract attention. "Mrs. Nagel, you haven't told anybody else the message—except your husband and us here?"

Us here?

"No, I haven't. But I think I should. I really think I should."

What's the message?

Bishop Gau said, "All right. Then I advise you to go ahead, Mrs. Nagel. Tell people of your experiences, and tell them the message, too."

"You're not advising *that!*" Monsignor Holstein was very upset.

"If silence is impossible, yes, I am," said Bishop Gau.

"Why not?" said Mrs. Nagel. "It's the truth, after all."

"No, *silence!*" cried Monsignor Holstein.

"No, the truth," said Bishop Gau. "It's the next-best thing. She can't go on like this. And we can't."

What's the message?

"You," said Monsignor Holstein, "*you* told me it was noncontroversial."

"I meant," replied Father Barnett, "in the political sense."

What's the message?

"'KEEP MINNESOTA GREEN'!" cried Monsignor Holstein, very upset. "What about the *rest* of the country? Or, for that matter, the *world?*"

Bishop Gau, swiftly rising from the desk, called upon the Bishop with a look and a nod, and stood with bowed head.

The Bishop, rising with an effort, responded with a prayer.

Mrs. Nagel did reveal the message to visitors, and consequently Mr. Nagel was less troubled by them, but life went on as before for the clergy concerned. Monsignor Holstein was very upset in April to hear that one of his ex-curates and one of the nuns from his parish school, whose union he had opposed, were being divorced in California, and in August Father Barnett was down with his back again. This took the Bishop to Fahrenheit again—quite a homecoming! He had continued with his livery-horsing, wasn't often seen at the Webb, and had put plenty of mileage on the Mercedes. He would have put on more if one day early in October, when the diocese was at its best and he was driving along U.S. 52, enjoying the scenery, he hadn't been sideswiped by a truck. He was in the hospital for a while, doing fairly well for a man of his age, he understood, until he took a turn for the worse.

PHARISEES

And he spake this parable unto certain which trusted in themselves that they were righteous, and despised others:

Two men went up into the temple to pray; the one a Pharisee, and the other a publican.

The Pharisee stood and prayed thus with himself, God, I thank thee, that I am not as other men are, extortioners, unjust, adulterers, or even as this publican.

I fast twice in the week, I give tithes of all that I possess.

And the publican, standing afar off, would not lift up so much as his eyes unto heaven, but smote upon his breast, saying, God be merciful to me a sinner.

—Luke 18:9–13

Taking a hard-boiled egg from the bowl on the bar, the publican—if he could be called that, for the joint was in his wife's name and he was now retired from his job as tax collector—squeezed it, trying to break the shell in his grip, and failed. So he held the egg down on the bar, rolled it back and forth, and in this manner broke the shell, which he removed. He sprinkled salt on the small end of the egg, and was eating this when a customer entered the joint.

"I see you're eating an egg," said the customer, an elderly Pharisee in a dark suit of conservative cut.

"I'm on this new diet," said the publican.

"What new diet is this, Walt?"

"It's this new cholesterol diet."

"Oh, yes. I've been hearing about it."

"In cholesterol, which I prefer to take in the form of eggs, I get all the things my body needs—animal fats, blood, nerve tissue, bile, to name but a few."

"Sounds good, Walt. Small brandy, please."

The publican was pouring a small brandy when a young thief entered the joint with a gun, saying, "This is a holdup."

While the holdup was in progress, another customer, an unfrocked Pharisee now engaged in community work, entered the joint, saying, "Hi, fellas. Hey, what's happening?"

"Watch it," said the young thief.

The ex-Pharisee then spoke to the young thief in a nice way, telling him that he could jeopardize his future in the community by such conduct, if, that is, he persisted in it.

"Maybe you're right," said the young thief sheepishly.

"I don't say I'm right. I don't say you're wrong," said the ex-Pharisee. "I try not to make value judgments. All I ask is that you think again. In the meantime, what'll you have, fella?"

"Just a beer."

"Two beers, Walt."

After serving them, the publican picked up the egg, which was eroding on the bar.

The Pharisee said, "Saw you this morning, Walt, unless my eyes deceived me."

"No, I was there. I was standing afar off."

"Walt, how is it I never see your wife there?"

"She's pretty busy."

"We're all pretty busy, Walt, but we can still find a few hours a day for the things that matter most."

"Such as?" said the ex-Pharisee.

"*We* were talking," said the Pharisee. "Walt and I."

"About what?" said the ex-Pharisee.

The publican leaned over the bar and, with a mouthful of egg, whispered, "Religion."

"Oh, *that*," said the ex-Pharisee.

A young woman, a dish, entered the joint rattling a can of coins. She approached the Pharisee with it.

"What's it for?" he asked.

"People."

The Pharisee shook his head. "I give tithes of all that I possess," he said.

"Oh, sure," said the dish, and rattled the can at the publican.

"My wife takes care of all that. She's off today."

"Oh, sure," said the dish.

"Hey, don't forget us," said the ex-Pharisee—who then folded a dollar and slipped it into the can.

The dish rattled the can at the young thief.

"We give at home," he said.

The ex-Pharisee slipped the young thief a five, which *he*, having seen how it was done, folded and slipped into the can, saying, "Now I see."

Watching the dish leave, the publican squeezed an egg, then rolled it on the bar, removed the shell, and salted the small end. "Want one?" he said to the Pharisee.

"Not today, Walt. Small brandy, please."

"Hey, what's happening?" said the ex-Pharisee. Going out into the entryway, where the dish was being attacked by rapists, he said, "Hi, fellas," and after apologizing for the young ex-thief, who had attacked one of the rapists from behind, he spoke to them all in a nice way, telling them that they could jeopardize their future in the community by such conduct, if, that is, they persisted in it. Not surprisingly, they all agreed.

The ex-Pharisee, the young ex-thief, the dish, and the six ex-rapists then repaired to the bar where they sat in a row, but could see each other in the mirror, all talking about poetry, music, drama, and better recreational facilities.

"Tired?" said the ex-Pharisee.

"A little," said the dish.

The young ex-thief said he'd be glad to go out with the can in her place, and offered to turn his gun over to her, the ex-Pharisee, or the ex-rapists, if that would make him more acceptable in her eyes, but that was not required of him, and he came back shortly with a full can.

"Don't thank me," he told the grateful dish. "Thank *him*."

The ex-Pharisee said, "You did it your way, fella."

The publican squeezed another egg, rolled it on the bar, removed the shell, salted the small end, and pointed it at the Pharisee invitingly.

"Not today, Walt. You see, I fast twice in the week, and this is one of my days."

"Big deal," said the ex-Pharisee. "I don't fast, and I don't give tithes, and I don't go to temple, and I thank God (if there is one) I'm not like the hypocrites that do!"

"And so say all of us," said one of the ex-rapists.

TINKERS

Not counting teddy bears and the like, they were seven
—two teen-age girls, two boys, seven and nine, a girl of
five, Mama, and Daddy—and after eight days over land
and sea, Daddy had a great desire to be out of the
public eye. So when they landed in Cobh, though they'd
intended to stay overnight there or in Cork, he phoned
the hotel in Ballydoo, near Dublin, and was happy to
hear that it would be all right to arrive that evening, a
day earlier than planned. At Dublin, the train, to their
surprise, became the boat train to Dun Laoghaire, and,
since Ballydoo lay in that direction, they stayed on it—
Daddy was happy to be saving a bit on taxi fares. At

Dun Laoghaire, he was happy not to have to take ship again, and to find a taxi big enough (he'd been thinking they'd need two) to accommodate them and their luggage. Things, it seemed to him—after the hotel in St. Paul, the heat in Chicago, the train trip to New York (who ever heard of washing your hair on a train?), the Empire State Building, Gimbel's, Schrafft's, Hammacher Schlemmer's (for compasses), and six days at sea—were looking up.

Except for overcrowding in the taxi, there was no difficulty until they reached their destination, almost. On the road, caught just in time by the taxi's headlights, there was a noisy gathering of some kind, around a two-tone horse.

"*Tinkers,*" the driver said with contempt, and proceeded slowly, half off the narrow pavement, while the tinkers and the horse, hoofs clonking, surged about in the dark.

"*Jem, don't sell that harse!*"

"*'M sellin' the bugger!*"

"Daddy," said the younger boy, who was sitting on Daddy's lap with Kitty, his stuffed cat, on his lap. "What's *wrong?*"

"Nothing's wrong. The man who owns the horse—his friend doesn't want him to sell it. That's all."

"Beebee'll buy it," said the older boy, who was sitting with Beebee, his teddy bear, on his lap, between Daddy and the driver, and gurgled at the thought of Beebee's wealth.

"Give it a rest," Daddy said.

Beebee, a millionaire (hotels, railroads, shipping, timber), had thrown his weight around on this trip—rather, had had it thrown around for him. When they checked into the hotel in New York, not a bad hotel, Daddy had been told, "Beebee usually stays at the Waldorf," and when they found their cabins on the

ship, "Beebee usually goes First Class," and in the dining room on the first night, "Beebee usually drinks
champagne"—and the wine steward, obviously a for-
eigner with ideas about American parents and children,
had to be told no, that was not an order. Mama and
Daddy were getting a little older, and had suffered a
little more on this trip.

It was not their first one to Ireland. They had gone
there for a year when the teen-agers were small, again
when the boys were smaller, and—the last time—the
youngest child had been born there. Each time, they
had rented a house in Ballydoo, and were hoping to do
so again. And this time they wouldn't have to settle for
what was immediately available, would be able to look
around for a while, because they would be staying on as
sole tenants of the hotel after it closed for the winter
and the proprietors, Major and Mrs. Maroon, went to
London. This arrangement, initiated by Irish friends,
had been concluded by correspondence, and since the
rent would be reasonable, and Mama and Daddy could
not recall a small hotel facing the harbor, they were
anxious to see it. When they did, they recalled it (them,
rather, these Victorian terrace houses, externally two,
now internally one), now the—though it, or they, looked
eastward to the sea—Westward Ho Hotel.

Without too much ado, Mrs. Maroon, a fiftyish out-
doors type, received and registered them as guests,
which they'd be for two weeks before coming into their
tenancy, and after they were shown their rooms and
given tea in the lounge (in the presence of two other
guests, women such as one sees in lounges in the British
Isles, one reading a book, one knitting), Major Maroon,
portly in a double-breasted blue serge jacket with one
of its brass buttons, a top one, missing, so that the five
remaining looked like the Big Dipper, appeared and
proposed billiards—to the boys.

"Oh, I don't know about *that*," Daddy said, rising, and, with visions of cues plowing up green pastures of cloth, accompanied the boys and Major Maroon, who smelled of stout, to what he called the Smoking Room and Library, which smelled of dog.

Billiards proved to be a form of skittles, the little table to be coin-operated. Major Maroon financed the first game, Daddy the second, after which he, having looked through the Library, a bookcase containing incunabula of the paperback revolution (Jeeves, Raffles) and Aer Lingus schedules for the previous summer but one (Take One), said it was past bedtime. "Ah, the lads'll like it here," said Major Maroon, and showed them where they'd find the cues.

Later that night, when the children were, it was to be hoped, asleep in their rooms, and Mama and Daddy were having a duty-free drink in theirs (no bar at the Westward Ho), Daddy mentioned the little coin-operated table.

Mama said severely, "It's something we'll have to watch."

And Daddy resented this—that she'd not only taken his point and given it back to him as her own, which was one of her conversational tricks, but that she had turned it against him in the process. He was touchy on this subject, the subject of thrift. He had been profligate in the past, yes, though badly handicapped by lack of wherewithal to be profligate with. But he had learned plenty from Mama in the years since their marriage, and while he still had plenty to learn about thrift, he did think it was time she forgot the past and saw him, if not as her equal, *as he was today*. He hadn't used shaving cream or lotion in years, and he hardly ever changed a blade. He always bought, *if* he bought, the economy size, and didn't take the manufacturer's word for it—had learned from Mama to weigh price against ounces. He saved string, wrapping paper, claret corks, and the parts of broken things that might come in handy, though many never did—pipestems, for instance. He kept the family in combs he found in the street and washed—how many fathers, not professional scavengers, did that? He had paid for only three deck chairs on the ship coming over. In Ireland, he always smoked pensioners' plug. In short, he was probably America's thriftiest living author. Yes, but—this was where he pooped out as a paterfamilias—he could not provide his loved ones with a lasting home. He had subjected them to too many moves, some presented as trips abroad, but still moves. And this one, at the other end, before they left, had been the worst to date.

The big old house they'd occupied as tenants had been sold, and the new owners, Mr. and Mrs. Stout, who planned to turn it into a barracks with bunk beds for college students, as they'd done with other big old houses in the neighborhood, had been underfoot constantly in the last thirty days—asking if it would be all right to have a few trees cut down; the front sidewalk taken up; the yard paved for parking; a notice posted at the college inviting students, possible occupants of the bunk beds, to drop around; and more, much more. It had been hard not to go along with all these requests, even though Mama and Daddy were free, legally, to reject them and were up to their ears in packing, for the Stouts were very pleasant people and were motivated, it seemed, by charity in their dirty work. "Golly, where will those poor kids park their cars?" Mama and Daddy had felt guilty about rejecting the paving project, even when the trees came crashing down. The Stouts had been too much.

Fifteen years earlier, when Mama and Daddy had begun their career as tenants and travelers, when they'd surrendered their house in the woods, the first and last place they'd owned, to the faceless men of the highway department for a service road, and a few years later, when they'd surrendered the beautiful old place, the oldest house in town, to the faceless men of the department of education for a parking lot (now occupied by a faceless building), there had been acrimony, arguments about the nature of progress, between usurpers and usurpees. This time, no. The Stouts, such pleasant people, had been too much. Mama and Daddy were still talking and, in the case of Mama, still dreaming about this move.

That night, at the Westward Ho, she suddenly said, "You know who *they* are?"

"Who *who* are?"

"The Maroons."

"How d'ya mean? Who *are* they?

"The Stouts."

"Oh, now, I wouldn't say that."

The hotel closed for the winter on schedule, but for some reason the Maroons were still there a week later. Mama and Daddy then heard from the youngest child, to whom Mrs. Maroon had confided, that London might not agree with Happy. (This was the *genius loci* of the Smoking Room and Library, a hairy terrier that looked like Ireland on the map when in motion, a very mixed-up dog, to judge by the way—ways, rather—it relieved itself.) So Mama and Daddy spoke up, and two days later the proprietors checked out.

Life in the hotel was then homier for the tenants in one respect than it had been in any house to date, in that they had a pet, but otherwise was much the same for them there as anywhere else they'd settled for a time. The children—the teen-agers attending school in Dublin, the younger ones in Ballydoo—had their new friends (the older boy often entertaining his at bil-

liards: it had occurred to Daddy but evidently not to
Major Maroon that it would be a good idea to leave the
tenants with the key to the little coin-operated table).
Mama, of course, had her shopping, cooking (in a
kitchen caked with grease), and her house- or hotel-
keeping. Daddy had his "office," a small room in the
uninhabited part of the hotel, where he read the *Irish
Times* and the *Daily Telegraph*, listened to the B.B.C.,
and did his writing.

He was between books, preparing to strike out in a
genre new to him. What he had in mind was a light-
hearted play, later to be a musical and a movie, about a
family of campers, possibly Germans, who, on arriving
in Ireland and wishing to do it right, would hire one of
those colorful horse-drawn caravans but make the mistake of pulling into a bivouac of tinkers for the night.
There would be singing, dancing, drinking, and fighting
around the campfire, a nice clash of life styles (*these*, in
the end, would be exchanged!) with plenty of love interest along the way—German boy, tinker girl, or vice
versa, maybe several of each for more love interest. He
couldn't overdo it, since he was writing for the theatre,
but there *were* problems. He knew nothing about
tinkers or Germans or, they might be, French, and if he
got them acting and talking right, would they, particularly the tinkers, be intelligible to an American audience? Would this audience—as it must—immediately
grasp what the Germans, French, or, they might be,
Japanese would not; namely, that the tinkers were not
proper campers like themselves? He was afraid he'd
have to do the whole damn thing in basic American
first, then do a vivid translation, thoughts of which,
since he was still in several minds as to the campers'
nationality (*Wunderbar! C'est magnifique! Banzai!*)
turned his stomach slightly. He had once read that nobody ever wrote a best seller, however bad, without

believing in it, but he doubted this, and even if it was true, he doubted that it was true of a smash-hit play, however bad. And what had struck him as a good idea for one ("This one will run and run") continued to do so.

But he wasn't getting on with it. Hoping to see or hear something he could use, perhaps another line of tinkerese to go with those he had ("A few coppers, sor," and, "I'll pray for you, m'lord"), he would take the train into Dublin, visit the junky auction rooms on the Quays, the secondhand bookshops, just wander around —too bad, what was happening to Dublin's fair city— and come home tired, with a few small purchases, always pastry from Bewley's, cherry buns, shortbread, barmbrack (at Halloween), or fruitcake (as Christmas approached).

This they'd have that evening in the lounge, some with tea, some with cocoa and wearing their pajamas— a nice family scene, yes, but one of those present was an impostor, Daddy would think, considering his responsibilities and how he'd shot the day. On some evenings, while Mama was reading aloud from Captain Marryat, one of the few clothbound authors in the Library, Daddy would have a new chapter from Beebee's family history to read, which was then in the writing and remarkable in one respect: the Beebee of the period (eighteenth century) had had a wife, children, and business associates with names like Kitty, Pussy, Toydy, Lion, Bear, Dragon, and Owl, whose present-day descendants were in precisely the same relationship to the present-day Beebee!

Stability, Daddy would think.

On some evenings, when the younger children were in bed and he was saying good night to them (another nice family scene) he would hear something to his credit, that the little girl liked living so close to the sea,

the boys so close to the trains—sea and trains thanks to
him, he'd think then, though the railway was now
owned by Beebee, he understood. He was wary of
Beebee. The millionaire had such a poor opinion of the
Westward Ho that he wouldn't buy it, he said—when
Beebee spoke, it was through the older boy, dryly,
rather like Mama's father—but Beebee wasn't in such
good shape himself. He was worn smooth in places, and
had a new nose (thanks to Mama) of different material,
which he was sensitive about, withdrawing from the
conversation if it was mentioned, as he did when frivo-
lous remarks were made about his extreme wealth.
"Well, good night, Millions," Daddy would say—and
might be told that Beebee (though present) was somewhere in the Indian Ocean, aboard *Butterscotch*, his
yacht, on a trip around the world, and on his return
would be buying new motorbikes for Lion and Bear,
who, being teen-agers, had crashed theirs. "On the
yacht?" "They're not with Beebee now. They radioed
him about it." "What'd Beebee say?" " 'Crazy kids. Just
have to buy 'em new ones.' " The older boy would
gurgle, and Daddy would shake his head in wonder at
Beebee's magnanimity. "Lion and Bear—they're back at
the ranch?" "Um." "That's the one in Colorado?" "Partly."
"It's a big ranch." "Um."

Daddy would then retire to the same room he and
Mama had occupied on the first night, where they now
had two relatively easy chairs and special lighting—
they now sat by two brass table lamps that he'd picked
up at an auction, instead of under the traditional bulb
suspended from the ceiling—and there, with the radio
and the electric fire playing between them, with their
reading matter and drinks, they'd spend the long evening.

By the middle of December, they were talking more
about their problem. They had looked at a couple of

houses that were too small, and one just not what they'd come to Ireland to live in (a thirties-period "villa" of poured concrete spattered with gravel—the agent had called it "pebbledash"), and one very nice place, "small Georgian," with a saint's well on the grounds, but unfurnished and rather remote *and*, it then came out, not for rent, the agent having presumed that they, as Americans, might buy it. That was all they'd done about their problem by the middle of December.

They weren't worried yet. They had the hotel, if need be, through January, and felt secure there, so secure that on some evenings they were inclined—at least Daddy was—to feel sorry for their homeowning friends in America. He wouldn't, he'd tell Mama, want to be Joe out there in the country, with the highway, perhaps, to be rerouted through his living room; or Fred by the river, with the threat of floods every spring (the American Forces Network, Europe, reporting six-foot drifts in the Midwest); or Dick in town, with that big frame house to paint every five years and those big old trees that, probably now heavy with snow and ice, might *not* fall away from the house if they fell.

One evening, after doing a spot of plumbing— Ireland, the land of welcomes, is also the land of running toilets—he told Mama that hard though it was to go through life making repairs in other people's houses and hotels, knowing that whatever you did you'd probably be doing again somewhere else, it was better than making repairs in your own home, knowing that THIS IS IT, that the repairs might well outlast you, or the dissolution of your household. This was one of the consolations of vagrancy that he hadn't heard about until he heard it from his own lips, and he liked it very much. Mama took exception to it.

One evening he told her that he'd heard a man on the B.B.C., on *Woman's Hour*, say that mobile families were superior families—and she took exception to it. He hadn't been listening carefully until it was too late, so couldn't give her the details, only remembered that mobile families were more . . . couldn't remember exactly what, only that they were superior, that the man, who was the spokesman for some association or group that had carried out a survey and issued a report, had said that mobile families were more . . .

"*More mobile?*"

One of her conversational tricks.

One morning, about a week before Christmas, they had a letter from Mrs. Maroon. She thanked them for sending on the mail, said that cabbages were very dear in London, and asked to be remembered, as her husband did, to the children and Happy. In a postscript, she said not to send on the mail for the time being, as she and her husband would be at the hotel shortly.

Mama and Daddy then had a lengthy discussion about "shortly," about whether it only meant *soon* or could conceivably mean *briefly.*

That evening, the Maroons returned.

Happy was glad to see them, and others were, too. "How long you staying?" the older boy asked them right away—a good question, but lost in the excitement. "*Daddy* calls Happy *Slap!*" the youngest child informed them, and Mama quickly offered them tea.

With the proprietors in residence again, the hotel wasn't what it had been for the tenants—their relationship to the dog, for instance, wasn't the same. No, even though proprietors and tenants went their own way, ate at opposite ends of the dining room, and in the evening at different times (like first and second sittings at sea, parents with small children at the first), it wasn't the same. And again, as before the proprietors left for London, there was a certain amount of overlap and flap in the kitchen. (Mama had once expected to have her very own.) Daddy was in trouble, too. After two days, he moved from the part of the hotel now occupied by the proprietors—lest his typing disturb them, his playing the radio during working hours scandalize them—to the part occupied by the tenants.

The next morning, in his new office, listening to *Music While You Work* on the B.B.C. and reading the *Irish Times* before getting to grips with the light-hearted play (in which the campers were now Americans), he came upon an item of professional interest to him: "County councils and urban district councils throughout Ireland are awaiting the publication of a report prepared by the Government Commission on Itineracy." Shouldn't that be Itinerancy? "It is expected that the report will contain several broad proposals for integrating itinerants into the normal life of the community. Their presence has often caused friction, particularly in Limerick and Dublin suburbs, where residents claim that they indulge in fighting and leave a large amount of litter." Yes, he'd seen some of it, and while the women, babes in arms, begged in the streets, the men, as somebody had said in a letter to the *Irish Times*, drank and played cards in a ditch. "During the winter, the tinkers usually camp at sites in these suburbs, or at sites in provincial towns, but some caravans stay on the road all the year round." Nothing new here, nothing for him. "There are six main tinker tribes." Oh? "The Stokeses, Joyces, MacDonaghs, Wards" . . . now, *wait* a minute . . . "and Redmonds."

So the odds against him were greater than he'd thought.

He took the next train into Dublin, left the *Irish Times* on it, and gave the first tinker woman he met a coin, wanting and not wanting to know her name.

On the Quays, he found some secondhand paperbacks for the younger children, and was tempted by a
copper-and-brass ship's lamp, not a reproduction and
not too big, to be auctioned that afternoon ("about half-
four," he was told). He bought a French paring knife
for Mama in a restaurant-supply place—he liked doing
business in such places.

He then had a pot of tea and two cherry buns at the
nearest Bewley's, selected a fruitcake, and, to pass the
time until half-four, just wandered around, window-
shopping and making a few small purchases: a couple
of ornaments for their Christmas tree, which was now
up in the lounge and rather bare; a tool, with a cloven
end and an attractive hardwood handle, to remove carpet tacks and also suitable for upholstery work, should
the need arise for him to do either; some brass screws
that might come in handy and were, in any case, nice to
have; a hardcover notebook (they did these very well in
the British Isles) such as he already had several of, with
inviting cream paper that he couldn't bring himself to
violate; more soft-lead (3B) pencils.

For some time, he stood looking in a seedsman's
window. Quite an idea, he thought, having a section of
a real tree there so one could see the various kinds of
branches, the various kinds of saws required to get at
them, saws shown cutting into them, and one, an ordinary carpenter's saw, shown cutting into a sign, just a
plank, that asked the question "WHY NOT HAVE THE SAW
FOR THE JOB?" Since on the property one might own
someday there would be many trees, wood being the
fuel of the future, and one would spend so much time
up on an extension ladder (shown) doing surgery, and
might otherwise fall and kill oneself, and with no insurance and six dependents, why not—except for the expense—have the saw for the job? (Beebee would.)

On the way back to the Quays, he booked two seats

to a coming play, and because the tickets hadn't been printed yet, and would be posted to him, he was asked to give his name and address (was suddenly sensitive about the former), and was told when he asked for a receipt, "Ah, that's all right." This he accepted, after a moment, remembering where he was (Ireland) and an attendant at this same theatre one night not undertaking to tap him on the shoulder when the time would come to leave (early, to catch the last train) but giving him his watch to hold. And also remembering the fruit huckster at the Curragh on Derby Day, short of change so early in the afternoon and on whose wares they'd lunched to economize, telling him to come back and pay later. And the bellboy at the old hotel in Dublin on their first visit to Ireland who, after making several trips up to their room to call them to the phone in the lobby (they were running an ad for a house), had politely declined to be tipped further for such service, which had continued. "Ah, that's all right." That was the beauty of, and the trouble with, Ireland.

He was early for the ship's lamp, and thought the prices made by the lots before it rather low, but saw right away that this was not going to be the case with the lot he wanted—a familiar feeling at auctions. He came into the bidding at the first pause, and after the figure he'd had in mind had been passed, the maximum figure, which was subject to revision in the event, he was still in it. And money talks! He arranged to take the ship's lamp with him, rather than come back for it the next day, saying he lived "down the country" and had to catch a train.

He returned to Ballydoo tired, took the short cut from the station, and entered the hotel by the rear, expecting to find Mama in the kitchen, but didn't. He assumed that something was taking too long in the oven. He went upstairs, expecting to find her in their

room having a glass of stout by the electric fire, and
perhaps reading the *Daily Telegraph*, but found her
lying on the bed, face down, in the cold and dark.

"What's *wrong?*"

"Look in the lounge."

"What d'ya mean?"

"Look in the lounge."

He threw a blanket over her, and hurried downstairs.

The younger children were in the lounge, as he'd
expected they would be, with the Christmas tree turned
on, but somebody else was there, too: a woman—he'd
seen her there before, three months before—knitting.

So Daddy, right away, got on the phone, and during the
second sitting (there wasn't a first one), with the help
of the local taximan, who also did light hauling, they
moved themselves and their effects, including groceries
and Christmas tree, out of the hotel and into a house
down the road. The agent was there, waiting for them
with a temporary lease, which was signed by flashlight
—the only hitch (a blow to Mama) was that the electricity was off in the house. But the agent had already
called the Electricity Supply Board, and the teen-agers,
who had been dispatched to the shop that kept open,
were soon back with a bundle of turf and a dozen
candles. And a candle, as Daddy pointed out, gives a
surprising amount of light for a candle. There was coal
in the shed, enough for two or three days, also kindling,
and the kitchen range only smoked at first. They had
their meal of baked beans and scrambled eggs by
candlelight in the kitchen. Then they had their dessert
—the fruitcake from Bewley's—by firelight in the parlor, some with tea, some with cocoa and wearing their

pajamas, and talking about the ship's lamp, which there hadn't been time to examine until then.

Mama explained its red and green windows and its internal parts—apparently all there except for the wick. Daddy was interested in the manufacturer's name and address (Telford, Grier & Mackay, Ltd., 16 Carrick St., Glasgow), almost invisible from polishing. He pointed out that copper and brass (and silver) looked better when slightly tarnished, better still when seen, as now, by firelight. No, he didn't know where the ship's lamp's *ship* was (the younger boy wanted to know), probably it *wasn't*, and no, didn't know what he was going to do with the ship's lamp. Just liked it, just liked looking at it, he said, and, seeing that that wasn't enough, said he might put it over the front door of the house they might have in America someday. They wouldn't have to worry about it, he said—these old ship's lamps were made to be out in all kinds of weather.

"Will we get to keep it, Daddy?" said the younger boy.

"Yes, of course."

"Daddy, he means the house," said one of the teenagers.

"Oh."

"The house in America," said the younger boy. "Will we get to keep *it*?"

"Yes, of course—when we get it." And Daddy remembered the paperbacks—one of them, actually, and then the others—still in his coat. Taking a candle, he went to the cloakroom (good idea, having a cloakroom in a house), and while there, heard a knock at the front door—hoped it was the Electricity Supply Board. It was a man in blue, a grey-haired *garda*, who had believed the house to be vacant, he said, until he saw the wee light from the fireplace.

"We're waiting for the E.S.B."

"Ah. You and the family were at the hotel, sir."

"We were, yes."

"And now you're here."

"We are, yes."

"And will you be here long, sir?"

"Six months. Have a six-month lease. May be here longer. Probably not. It's hard to say. We never know."

"Ah, indeed. We never know. Good night, sir."

No, not the E.S.B., Daddy said, returning to the parlor, and gave the younger children the paperbacks, saying of one (*The Market: The Buying and Selling of Shares*, in which subject the older boy had shown an encouraging interest—Beebee's influence?), "If you have any questions, ask Millions." And noticed how quiet it was then, so quiet the turf could be heard burning, puffing.

"Beebee's gone," said the youngest child.

Daddy looked at the older boy.

"Sold Beebee."

"Now, *wait* a minute."

"A friend wanted to buy him. One of my friends."

It was painful to hear the pride in the boy's voice, in having friends, and Daddy knew what Mama was thinking, that this is what comes from being a mobile family. "*What* friend? What's his *name*? Where's he *live*? What *kind* of boy is he? Do *I* know him? It doesn't matter. You can't *sell* Beebee."

"I can always buy him back. That's part of the deal."

"*You can't sell Beebee.* Go get him. *Now.*"

"In the morning," Mama said.

"No, *now.*"

"He's got his pajamas on," Mama said.

"He can take 'em off."

Mama said nothing.

"O.K., *I'll* go."

So Daddy went, and at the friend's house, a cottage, did *not* say that the older boy missed his teddy bear, or that others did, but still told the truth. "Beebee was a gift from my mother"—his mother whose funeral he, in Ireland then, had been too broke to attend—"and I don't think she'd like it if he left us." The friend, his mother, his older sister, his two small brothers, they all seemed to understand. No trouble. Ten bob. And after a cup of tea, Daddy and Beebee—who looked the same, grumpy, stuffy, and still sure of himself—came home.

The electricity was on when they got there, the Christmas tree was going, and the younger children were in bed.

When Daddy put Beebee in with the older boy and said, "Good night, Millions," there was a gurgle in the dark that made him wonder if he'd been taken.

"Where's the money?"

"Spent it."

"*What?* Already? All of it? On *what?*"

"Billiards."

Mama and Daddy had work to do, but were tired, and spent the evening in the parlor before the fire (it and the tree gave enough light to talk by), with their drinks. There hadn't been time until then for him to tell her what Mrs. Maroon had said: that it hadn't originally been the plan to open the hotel for the Christmas season, that unforeseen requests for bookings (she had thanked him again for sending on the mail) and the dearness of things in London had combined to change the plan, and that she and her husband had hesitated to inform the tenants, for fear of upsetting them.

"We're well out of that," he said.

"Yes," she said.

They talked about the house, about the carved mahogany chimney piece, which, though, was spoiled by the glazed tiles (these reminding him of the Men's Room at the Union Station in Chicago), and about what they'd need in the way of equipment—different plugs for the brass lamps, for instance, for there were a number of types in use in Ireland and they had the wrong type for this house, which, though, had to be expected.

"The odds are three or four to one against you whenever you move," he said.

"Yes," she said.

He tuned in the American Forces Network, Europe, for the home news, and heard that there was a blizzard sweeping across the Midwest. Then "Mr. Midnight" came on with his usual drivel about "music for night people, romance, and quiet listening . . . lonesome sounds of a metropolitan city after dark"—and they discussed "metropolitan city," Mama saying that it was redundant, Daddy that he didn't like the sound of it but pointing out that it might not be redundant in certain circumstances, citing bishops who were metropolitans, whose seats, sees, or see cities, were rightly called metropolitan seats, sees, or cities. But Mama still took exception to it.

After that, they talked—he did—about their friends in America, about Joe and the highway, about Fred and the river, more about Dick and those big old trees that were probably heavy with snow and ice now, and about that big frame house that had to be painted every five years.

"That's one good thing about a house like this," he said. "Pebbledash."

"Yes," she said.

A NOTE ON THE TYPE

The text of this book was set on the Linotype in a face called Primer, designed by Rudolph Ruzicka, who was earlier responsible for the design of Fairfield and Fairfield Medium, Linotype faces whose virtues have for some time now been accorded wide recognition.

The complete range of sizes of Primer was first made available in 1954, although the pilot size of 12-point was ready as early as 1951. The design of the face makes general reference to Linotype Century—long a serviceable type, totally lacking in manner or frills of any kind—but brilliantly corrects its characterless quality.

Composed by Maryland Linotype Composition Co., Baltimore, Maryland. Printed and bound by American Book-Stratford Press, Saddle Brook, New Jersey.

Typography and binding design by Susan Mitchell.